D0341181

ALSO BY RICHARD PAUL EVANS

THE MISTLETOE COLLECTION

The Mistletoe Promise

The Mistletoe Inn

The Mistletoe Secret

THE NOEL COLLECTION

The Noel Diary

The Noel Stranger

THE WALK SERIES

The Walk

Miles to Go

The Road to Grace

A Step of Faith

Walking on Water

THE BROKEN ROAD TRILOGY

The Broken Road

The Forgotten Road

The Four Doors

A Winter Dream

Lost December

Promise Me

The Christmas List

Grace

The Gift

Finding Noel

The Sunflower

A Perfect Day

The Last Promise

The Christmas Box Miracle

The Carousel

The Looking Glass

The Locket

The Letter

Timepiece

The Christmas Box

FOR CHILDREN AND YOUNG ADULTS

The Dance

The Christmas Candle

The Spyglass

The Tower

The Light of Christmas

THE MICHAEL VEY SERIES

Michael Vey: The Prisoner of Cell 25

Michael Vey 2: Rise of the Elgen

Michael Vey 3: Battle of the Ampere

Michael Vey 4: Hunt for Jade Dragon

Michael Vey 5: Storm of Lightning

Michael Vey 6: Fall of Hades

Michael Vey 7: The Final Spark

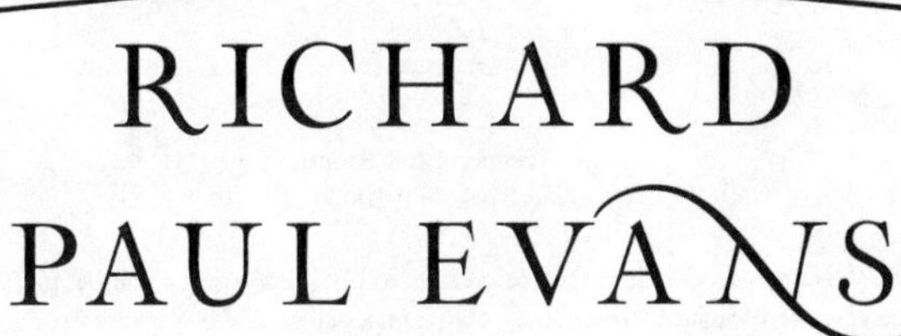

The Road Home

SIMON & SCHUSTER

New York London Toronto Sydney New Delhi

Simon & Schuster
1230 Avenue of the Americas
New York, NY 10020

First Simon & Schuster hardcover edition May 2019

Manufactured in the United States of America

1 3 5 7 9 10 8 6 4 2

Library of Congress Cataloging-in-Publication Data
Names: Evans, Richard Paul, author.
Title: The road home / Richard Paul Evans.
Description: First Simon & Shuster hardcover edition. | New York : Simon & Schuster, 2019. | Series: The broken road trilogy ; book 3
Identifiers: LCCN 2019007757 (print) | LCCN 2019008744 (ebook) | ISBN 9781501111846 (ebook) | ISBN 9781501111822 (hardback) | ISBN 9781501111839 (trade paperback)
Subjects: | BISAC: FICTION / Christian / Romance. | FICTION / Romance / Contemporary. | GSAFD: Christian fiction. | Road fiction.
Classification: LCC PS3555.V259 (ebook) | LCC PS3555.V259 R62 2019 (print) | DDC 813/.54—dc23
LC record available at https://lccn.loc.gov/2019007757

ISBN 978-1-5011-1182-2
ISBN 978-1-5011-1184-6 (ebook)

Photograph on page 86 is courtesy of the author.

To David Welch. A remarkable father.

The Road Home

Author's Note

Dear reader,

This is my third and final book about the man you've come to know as Charles James and his walk across the famous Route 66. Perhaps more interesting than his literal walk is his walk from his previous self. It's like they say: it's not the road that changes, it's the traveler.

It was during this phase of his journey that I met him at the Wagon Wheel Restaurant in the blistering heat of Needles, California. At that point neither of us knew how his story would end. Now I do. Truth is more incredible than fiction.

This final volume begins in Amarillo, Texas, about halfway along Route 66. Again, per our agreement, I've allowed him to tell his story in his own words. What you choose to believe is up to you.

Chapter One

I've come to believe that direction is more important than destination. It's better to be in hell looking up toward heaven than it is the other way around.

CHARLES JAMES'S DIARY

FROM CHARLES JAMES

When I was eight years old, about five years before I dismissed God from my life, I asked the priest at church if God made the Garden of Eden.

"God made everything," he replied.

"Did he make the snake, too?"

Even though my question was an honest one, the priest shook his head angrily and called me a naysayer. At that age I had no idea what that meant, but from his tone, I was sure it was something sinful.

More than twenty years later I still haven't stopped thinking about that question. Perhaps the truth is that it's impossible to build an Eden without snakes, because there's a snake inside all of us.

Likewise, I've come to believe that you can't have order without chaos. That doesn't mean that chaos is desirable or on equal terms with order. The nature and goal of civilization is to bring order to chaos (hence the word "civil"). But I don't see how you can have one without the other. Even anarchy follows rules.

My life right now is the perfect example of that conundrum. I'm living on the street with my future unknown, my business closed down, walking to a woman who not only believes I'm dead but might also not even be upset that I am. My life is the epitome of chaos. So why does my life feel more in order than it has in a decade? Maybe because, in the end, where we are is less important than where we're going.

Chapter Two

On the road again. Blisters and fatigue. Willie Nelson made it sound much nicer.

CHARLES JAMES'S DIARY

One thousand eighty-nine miles, give or take a few steps. That's how much farther it was to the end of Route 66. That's three and a half states: Texas, New Mexico, Arizona, and California.

I started my walk eighty-two days ago. The reason that had initially driven my walk, at least in part, was now gone. I was taking my self-imposed walk of shame back to my ex-wife, Monica, hoping to win her back. Yesterday I learned that she's getting married. I have lost her twice.

I suppose "lost" isn't really the right word. I had given her away. It was one of a million mistakes in my life, but also by far the biggest. I wondered who the lucky man was. I hoped that he was better than me. She deserved that.

In the meantime, I still had 1,100 miles to walk. At least I had time to think. Few things clear the mind like walking. And I still had a lot of mind clearing to do.

I got up early the next morning. The respite with Amanda had been nice, especially after the time I'd spent working the fields with the migrant workers, but I was ready to get back on the road. While my journey remained the same, my destination had changed. I thought (or hoped) I might be settling in Santa Monica. Now Santa Monica was nothing more than a finish line, the mountain's pinnacle; and once I reached the summit, there would be nothing to do but go back down. Back home. Wherever that was these days.

I ate breakfast in the Marriott hotel's restaurant, then slung on my pack and walked back out into the warm Texas air. The walking was pleasant, or at least it would have been had my heart not ached so much.

It was nearly two hours before I reached the outskirts of Amarillo. A long strip of road laid claim to Route 66—although the road itself took on several different names—and the street was lined with signs, route-themed stores, and more Route 66 markers than I'd seen during my whole time in Texas. The last name the street took was West Amarillo Boulevard, where I got back onto the interstate and exited the Amarillo city limits.

I took a slight detour off 66 to see one of the most famous stops on the route—the notorious Cadillac Ranch, a peculiar landmark consisting of ten vintage Cadillacs buried nose-first in the ground in a rutted cow pasture, their tails in the air like posturing stink bugs.

The Cadillacs, ever changing from visitors' participation (and spray cans), are brightly colored with layers of graffiti so thick that the cars' surfaces almost feel plastic. The site's architects had called their work an "interactive monument," though I don't know if it had started that way or if they had, through time, succumbed to the inevitable.

Since the monument's unveiling, the cars had been painted about every color in a crayon box, including all pink—to honor the financer's wife's birthday—and all black, to mark the death of the artist. The cars were even once restored to their original painted colors by a national hotel chain as part of a Route 66 landmark restoration project. Predictably, the restored cars, and even the plaque that honored the event, went less than twenty-four hours before both were covered with graffiti.

The pasture was fenced off in either direction as far as I could see, with a single, well-established opening a little north of the cars. There was a sign hanging on the fence that read,

THIS IS NOT A STATE PARK.

NO LITTERING.

(Which begs the question, does that mean that you're expected to litter at state parks?)

In spite of the sign, there was litter everywhere, and

the predominant features of the landmark, apart from the Cadillacs themselves, were the piles of emptied spray-paint cans that surrounded the cars.

There were only half a dozen people at the site, including a man parked along the road selling Route 66 souvenirs and Cadillac Ranch bumper stickers.

There was a strangely decorated car parked about ten yards west of the fenced entryway. It was a Ford Bronco that had been accessorized with strings of lights, plastic skeleton figurines, and thousands of rhinestones. Its grille was adorned with a winged skeleton wearing a tiara, and the hood was covered with rhinestones in the shape of a skull encircled by black rubber mice. On the roof of the car was a skeleton village with at least a hundred small plastic skeletons surrounded by painted lace and more rhinestones, all of it intertwined with LED lights.

Standing next to the car was a woman I guessed to be its owner. She was as flamboyant as the vehicle. Her hot-pink hair was adorned with a saucer-sized white silk flower, and tattoos covered nearly all visible flesh.

Next to her was another woman similarly inked but differently adorned, wearing a Stetson hat and a sheer, white-lace sundress with a red silk cummerbund. She was cradling a small, fluffy white dog.

"Nice car," I said. I assumed that anyone who went to that much work clearly wanted her car to be noticed.

The woman smiled. "Thank you."

"Did you do this yourself?"

She nodded. "It's how I roll," she said, relishing the pun. "I'm a *cartist.*"

"Cartist," I repeated. "Clever."

"Our cars are our canvases. This is my third art car."

I looked out over the painted Cadillacs in the field. I supposed they were art cars, too. "Like the Cadillacs."

"Except ours still run."

I shouldn't have been too surprised that someone had taken automotive self-expression to this limit. Americans have always expressed themselves through their automobiles—from the macho signaling of muscle cars to the snooty elitism of Rolls-Royces.

"Where are you from?"

"Toronto."

"You drove all the way from Toronto to see this?"

"No. We came down for an art car show in Houston. It's a big art-car town."

"There are other . . . cartists?" I asked.

"There are thousands of us. There's even a school for it."

"We have a newsletter," the red-sashed woman proudly interjected. "It's a society. Last month we went to a show near Durango, Colorado. The prisoners decorated three cars. We drove our cars outside the fences so the inmates could see. It was quite a parade."

"I can only imagine," I said, which was true. "Good luck. I hope you don't lose any of your skeletons on the way."

"I've got more."

"Boxes of them," the cummerbund woman mumbled.

The Cadillacs were about a hundred yards from the road. Besides me, there were now just two other people: a foreign couple taking pictures of each other. The man was tall and lanky with blond hair, the woman tall and voluptuous. They kept switching positions as they took their pictures, speaking in a language I didn't recognize.

"Would you like me to take your picture?" I asked.

The man turned to me, then said in a thick accent, "Yes. Thank you much." He handed me his phone, then walked back and put his arm around the woman. I took about a dozen pictures and handed their phone back.

"*Tak*," he said, which I assumed meant thank you, or some variant of it.

I walked down the row of cars. There were ten in all, buried, I read, at the same angle as the Pyramids of Giza.

Initially the monument had started as a display of the evolution of automobile tail fins, starting with the 1949 Caddie and going up to 1963—the fins of the late fifties being the most dramatic of the collection before diminishing into nothing.

I sorted through a pile of discarded paint cans before I found one that still had something left in it—a can of neon orange paint. I shook the can, then walked up to the last car and wrote in large letters,

CHARLES JAMES LIVES

I tossed the can back on the ground with the rest of its family. I wondered if anyone would notice or consider what I wrote before spraying over it with their own message.

I walked back out to the road. The skeleton-mobile was gone.

Chapter Three

Abandoned buildings along an abandoned road stand (barely) as a testament to the truth that nothing this side of heaven lasts forever.

CHARLES JAMES'S DIARY

Less than a mile from Cadillac Ranch I passed a hand-painted sign that read:

BATES MOTEL

Each room with a shower

and knife sharpener.

I wasn't sure if the motel existed or not, and I made a mental note to check into it the next time I had Internet, but I never did. I got back on the southern frontage road, stepping over a dead rattlesnake as I crossed. On both sides of me were windmills and oil wells suckling from mother earth.

About a dozen miles into the day I came to a street sign pointing to an original section of Route 66. I crossed north under Interstate 40 to the frontage road and onto 66, where the Route's shield was painted on the asphalt.

Late that afternoon I reached the town of Wildorado. It stunk. Literally. It wasn't until I had walked through a dozen cities that it occurred to me that towns have smells as distinct as humans do. I could tell you if I were in New York or Chicago by the smell. But this town's odor was more than a curiosity; it was an unbearable stench. If I'd had a window, I would have rolled it up and turned off the air conditioner. The place smelled like a stockyard, which it was. I don't mean this as an insult to Wildorado's few but hardy residents. Sympathy, really. Sympathy bordering on admiration. It would take a strong human to live in such a place. Or at least someone who was olfactorily challenged. (Nose blind? Nose deaf? Is there a word describing the malfunction of this sensory organ?) I tied my shirt around my lower face like a bank robber.

Near the stockyard was a café appropriately named

The Windy Cow Café

Not surprisingly, it was out of business. Next to it was an old, weathered billboard that read

When Trouble Calls on You, Call On God

I spotted a motel sign in the distance, which I was glad for because I was ready to stop for the day. As I neared the sign, I saw that the motel was, like the café, out of business. The asphalt parking lot was as cracked as a dropped platter, with two- to three-foot saplings eagerly pushing up out of the crevices.

The building itself was white bricked with dusty blue doorjambs and red posts holding an overhanging roof, which, in spite of the supports, sagged in places.

As I walked around the motel, I found that many of the windows were still intact. In fact, some of the rooms were in unexpectedly good condition, with clean hardwood floors, doormats, and framed pictures still on the walls.

The beds had been removed, but even the bathrooms were in fair condition. I flushed a toilet and it worked, which I considered a luxury. The door on the first room I chose wouldn't close, so I went to the next. There were an air conditioner and wall-mounted light fixtures but no power.

Hanging on the wall was a wood-framed picture of a red barn—the kind of art one finds in the back aisle of a dollar store. On the ground beneath it was a lacy pink bra and a water-damaged phone book.

I sat on the floor and ate a dinner of two cans of cold SpaghettiOs, turkey jerky, an apple, and half a round of hard-crusted bread. I laid out my cushion and sleeping bag in the middle of the room, then drew the drapes and locked the door. I couldn't smell the stockyard, just the pungent smell of mildewed drywall. I fell asleep quickly.

I had a strange dream that night. I dreamt that I woke and there was a young boy standing in the doorway looking at me. It shook me up. I hope it was a dream.

Chapter Four

Today I reached the halfway point of my journey. Still 1,139 miles to go. A million more miles in my heart.

CHARLES JAMES'S DIARY

Dream aside, I slept well. I packed up at sunrise and continued my walk along the south side of I-40. Walking was flat and easy with the oncoming traffic to my right. I had started early, as I wanted to reach the town of Adrian before it closed—which I was getting used to in these small towns. Adrian was widely accepted as the halfway mark on Route 66.

Outside of the freeway traffic, I passed hardly anyone that morning besides a man cutting weeds along the side of the road with a mower attached to the back of a John Deere tractor. It reminded me of a story my grandfather had told me when I was young. The bale trailer he dragged behind the John Deere he drove (none of my family ever owned the big equipment they used) was named by its inventor the Harobed—a peculiar name that was later revealed to be the inventor's daughter's name, Deborah, spelled backward. The inventor actually had two daughters, the second being named Lana, whose name, for obvious reasons, wouldn't have worked as well.

In midmorning I reached the town of Vega, passing a rusted-out, antique Ford truck strategically placed next to a pristine Old Route 66 sign. Vega was one of the towns that had also laid claim to be the halfway mark on Route 66, but, from all accounts, it hadn't taken. That's not to say that Vega wasn't halfway. It likely was. The real question was, halfway on which version of Route 66? The road had changed so much over the years that several towns could legitimately claim the title.

Vega was a thriving town with a football field and working granaries. Not far past the city sign, I stopped at the Hickory Inn Café to eat breakfast. All the vehicles in the parking lot were trucks.

That afternoon, I walked past miles of wind farms, the stark white towers rising against the horizon like silent, swatting giants. Every town I passed that day had two things: granary silos and wind turbines.

A little after noon I reached the town of Landergin. There was nothing there of note—a modern ghost town. I walked on at a faster pace, driven to reach the first real milestone of my journey.

I reached Adrian at half past one, the landmark heralded by a large sign on the north side of the road that read *Midpoint*, with a two-pointed arrow, one end pointing toward Los Angeles—1,139 miles—the other east toward Chicago, with the same figure.

I stood in front of the sign for a few minutes and let it sink in.

ADRIAN, TEXAS

MIDPOINT

LOS ANGELES CHICAGO

1139 MILES ⟷ 1139 MILES

On the opposite side of the road was the Midpoint Café. I crossed the street to it. The sign on the door said that the café was only open until two, and it was already 1:45. I walked inside hoping they would still serve me, or at least sell me something to take out.

The diner was a colorful, retro-styled eatery reminiscent of the Route's heyday, with painted white cinderblock walls and neon signage, an old Coca-Cola dispenser and a matching chest refrigerator, vintage advertisements, and a neon-tubed jukebox. The wall was lined with booths with black vinyl seats with red piping like the original Batmobile.

Above the dining room were slow-turning ceiling fans, and the entryway floor was tiled in black-and-white squares like a large checkerboard. There was a narrow soda counter next to the kitchen with vinyl and chrome bar stools and a whiteboard above it advertising, in handwritten scrawl, a selection of pies and soups du jour. There were maybe a dozen other diners in the room.

A pleasant-looking woman in her early forties walked out to greet me. She wore a Route 66 T-shirt and a badge that read CARRIE.

"Just one?" she asked.

"Just me."

She led me over to a booth in the corner. "How's this?"

"Perfect," I said. "I'm not too late?"

"We're easy. We pretty much stay open as long as we have customers. Unless the cook has something important." She grinned. "And he never has anything important." She handed me a menu. "Would you like something to drink?"

"I'll have one of those Route 66 sodas," I said. "To celebrate midpoint. The blue one."

"Blu Razzberri," she said. "I like those."

"And some water. Lots of water."

"I'll bring you a pitcher." She turned and walked back to the kitchen. I surveyed the room's occupants, which appeared to be as geographically eclectic as the international terminal at O'Hare. The couple next to me was speaking Italian, some of which I understood. (I dated a model from Milan for a few years.) The woman was flirting and teasing the man about his *naso grande*. On the west side of the dining room was an opening to a gift shop.

My waitress returned with my beverages. "Do you know what you'd like to eat?"

I set down the menu. "What do you like to eat?"

"Since you asked, the best thing I've had lately isn't on the menu. I had a grilled cheese and green chili sandwich with a cup of tomato soup."

"That sounds good," I said. "Only make it two sandwiches and a bowl."

"You've got a healthy appetite for someone so thin."

"I need the calories," I said. "I'm walking Route 66."

"That would do it," she said. "That's a lot of calories."

I glanced around. "How many of your diners are traveling the Route?"

"Probably three-fourths. But in all my years here, I've only met three people walking. One of them had a goat with him."

"I've heard of the goat walker."

"He was carrying his goat in a wagon."

"I heard that, too."

"Go figure," she said, shaking her head. "I'll put your order in."

Less than ten minutes later she returned with the grilled cheddar with chilis.

"How long have you worked here?" I asked.

"About five years. But we bought the place two years ago. My mother, my sister, and me."

"So you're the owner."

"One of them."

"That's why you don't close when there's still business to be had," I said. "And how is business?"

"It's been good. I meet a lot of interesting people. That guy, William . . ." she stopped. "The guy who played Captain Kirk on *Star Trek* . . . he does travel commercials now."

"William Shatner," I said.

"Right, Shatner. He ate here once."

"What did he eat?"

"I don't remember. I just remember he loved my mother's pie. He made a big fuss about it. Left my mom a hundred-dollar tip."

"That must have been some pie."

"My mom's famous for her Ugly Pie."

"What's Ugly Pie?"

"It's something we inherited. Our pies were originally called Midpoint Ugly Crust Pies, but it was eventually just abbreviated to Ugly Pies."

"What's the favorite flavor?"

"Believe it or not, it's Elvis's Chocolate-Peanut-Butter-Banana Pie."

"Sounds a little disgusting," I said. "But it is Elvis."

"Everyone loves Elvis," she agreed.

"I'll try a piece with some coffee and milk."

"You got it." She walked away, returning a few minutes later with a large piece of pie.

"Is the Fabulous 40 motel next door open?" I asked.

"They were this morning."

"Do they have room service?"

"No. They have a café, but it's closed for remodeling."

"Is there anywhere else to eat? A grocery store?"

"Not in Adrian."

"Then I'd better get something for dinner. What pies do you have left?"

"Just about everything. I'd recommend the apple or whiskey pecan."

"How about one of each and a chopped brisket sandwich to go?"

"We're out of the brisket, but our pulled pork is good. Personally, I think it's better."

"Then I'll have that. And some of your chicken noodle soup."

She took out a pad and wrote down my order. "I'm pretty sure they have a microwave at the hotel," she said. "If not, Sheila will warm it up for you."

"Thank you."

By the time I finished eating my lunch I was the last one in the café. Carrie had taken off her apron and brought over a large sack with my dinner. "I put in a chicken salad sandwich, too," she said. "Someone ordered one a half hour ago and then changed their mind."

I paid the bill, leaving her a twenty-dollar tip, then walked over to the Fabulous 40 motel, which had changed its name after Route 66 was replaced by I-40. It was a nondescript building, clean and hospitable. The motel sign was a Route 66 classic, but the neon was in bad condition. Apparently there had been a hailstorm that had damaged the sign's tubing.

Their diner, which was closed, was called the Bent Door because the entryway door and door frame were, in fact, bent forward at a 140-degree angle.

That night, as I lay in bed, the reality of where I was hit me. I was halfway through my walk. In a sense, there was no turning back. Not that I was considering it, but at least now there was no point to it. It's like the story of the man who swam halfway across the English Channel before deciding he couldn't make it and swam back.

A lot had changed since I left Chicago, but most of all was myself. I felt different about myself. Ironically, I think I felt better about myself because I felt worse about myself. I know that might not seem to make any sense, but it does. Especially for a narcissist.

I can admit now that I was, maybe still am, a narcissist. I once believed, like my fellow narcissists, that I was not insecure, when the opposite was glaringly true. During one of our therapy sessions in Chicago, my therapist, Jennifer, told me that everyone has, to some degree, a subconscious belief in their own worthlessness. Narcissists have the same feelings, but instead of acknowledging them, they cover them up with a delusional denial of all wrongdoing. That was me. That was the core of my mantra, "There is no God but me."

But now I was exhausted from the constant mental acrobatics required to make myself believe I was "God," or even "good." It was incredibly liberating to finally admit that I was seriously flawed, and that I, like the rest of humanity, was a sinner.

That night, I took a long bath and then ate my pie, my sandwiches, and my soup, in that order. Then I lay back, watched some TV, and went to sleep.

Chapter Five

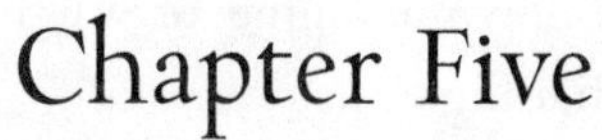

Today I reached New Mexico.
Nothing to see, and all day to see it.

CHARLES JAMES'S DIARY

I woke the next morning thinking of my family. I'm not sure why they'd suddenly emerged in my consciousness. Maybe they were always there, just below surface like groundwater. The truth was, I had relegated that part of my life to the past—like reruns on television—when the actors in that drama had, no doubt, moved on to play new roles.

It had been years since I'd seen any of them. My father was the last one I'd seen, and my visit with him had been horrific. Considering his perpetual bitterness and anger, I wasn't surprised at the trajectory his life had taken. He was broken both physically and emotionally.

I had learned then that my mother had divorced him. I was neither surprised nor disappointed by this. But their divorce wasn't only an end, it was also a beginning. Where was my mother now? Had she left Utah? Had she remarried? Did she follow me online, or was I dead to her before I died on that flight?

And then there was my younger brother, Mike. Thinking of him always brought a twang of guilt. He was a teenager when I left. He had begged me not to leave, but I did anyway. He was a man now. For all I knew, he could be married. *Does he hate me?* I wondered what he would have to say when I saw him again. I wondered if I ever would see him again.

Maybe I had thought of them because I'd reached a pivotal point in my walk where the end was foreseeable. As I rebuilt my life, I sensed that they, too, would play a part in that process.

I ate breakfast at the Midpoint Café. Carrie was again working and, like the day before, was pleasant, but we didn't talk as much, as the place was slammed and she was running from booth to booth like a baseball player caught in a hot box. I was glad they were busy. I wanted the café to do well. I wanted Carrie to do well.

I had coffee, biscuits with sausage gravy, and two Texas-sized pancakes with enough butter to clog a drainpipe, or at least my arteries. I wasn't in any great hurry, and I enjoyed the meal. I drank a refill of coffee, thanked Carrie, who wished me well, and then went back to the road.

Other than the wind farms, there was nothing to see for the next ten miles. I felt like I was living in one of those cartoons where the landscape just keeps repeating itself. When I reached the oddly named Deaf Smith

County, the original Route 66 road appeared again, but it ended only a mile later.

By late afternoon I reached the town of Glenrio, a town divided by state borders. It was another Route 66 locale that had been killed by the construction of the new interstate. Ahead of me was the enthusiastic state sign:

NEW MEXICO!

"LAND OF ENCHANTMENT"

(I've always been a little suspect of states that put exclamation points after their name. An English teacher once told me to never use exclamation points. "If you have to use one," she said, "what you're writing doesn't deserve one.")

Three more states to go. Just a few miles past the border was Russell's Truck and Travel Center. It was a large and solitary compound—an oasis in the desert. It had everything I needed: a store well stocked with supplies and sundries, a restaurant, a coin laundry, hot showers, and a lounge with television.

The best part of the travel center was the free car museum, which had some of the most beautiful restored cars I had ever seen, including a pink 1957 T-bird convertible. The sign in front of it read:

A CLASSIC CAR

IS LIKE A MAN'S WIFE—

LOOK BUT DON'T TOUCH

THANK YOU

Vintage automobiles were not the only collectibles on display. There was a collection featuring the evolution of Coca-Cola vending machines, a large case of authentic cowboy spurs, and even a Big Boy figurine from the restaurant chain.

I spent an hour in the museum. There were definitely some cars I would love to add to my collection if I ever got back into that kind of thing.

I ate dinner at the center's Route 66 Diner—an all-you-can-eat catfish platter with grilled shrimp in crawfish creole sauce. Then I took a long shower in their hospitality center.

I put my clothes in the washer, then, with the manager's permission, set up my tent near their RV lot. I then went back inside and watched television until my clothes were dried and it was time for bed.

I woke early the next morning to the sound of diesel trucks starting their engines. The heavy, synchronized roar sounded like the start of the Daytona 500.

The sun had just emerged over the eastern horizon, and I could hear the sound of truckers speaking to each other in their cultish language.

What a haul, started in Queen City and there was nothing but dragonflies and brown wrappers with Ko-

daks, hardly doin' double nickels. Wouldn't have made it to this choke-and-puke if it weren't for a rookie bear bait, ice breakin' for me clean to Big A.

I packed up my things and went back inside the travel center and ate a large breakfast—the Trucker's Big Steak Omelet, coffee, and apple juice—then filled my pack with supplies and started back out again.

Besides a stop in the small town of San Jon for water, there wasn't much of anything except road in this stretch of New Mexico. The skies grew increasingly threatening, and around two I felt some drops of rain, which started to increase. The only shelter in sight was an abandoned filling station, and I hurried to it. The door was locked, but the glass had been broken out of it. I climbed in through the open frame.

The room smelled moldy but was not entirely unwelcoming. I laid out my tent on the floor and lay back on it, resting my head on my pack, waiting for the rain to stop. It didn't. I had a simple dinner of salami, rolls, and a beer from the travel center, then lay back and fell asleep to the sound of water dripping around me.

Chapter Six

Churchill said, "If you're walking through hell, keep walking." I say, "Drink a lot of water and run like hell."

CHARLES JAMES'S DIARY

The sky was clear the next morning but the ground was muddy. I ate some jerky and dried banana chips and apricots for breakfast, then went back out, walking only on asphalt. Of all the places I'd walked, this stretch was perhaps the most barren, which is really saying something. The only structures I encountered had long been abandoned and then reclaimed by wilderness.*

My next destination was the town of Tucumcari, about

* I'm surprised at how quickly the wilderness reclaims itself. When the entire town of Chernobyl, Ukraine, was evacuated, we got an idea of how long things lasted. Within just a few decades, the roads were destroyed, buildings had collapsed, and packs of wild dogs roamed the streets like in an apocalyptic nightmare.

twenty miles from where I'd spent the night. I passed more than a few hotels, including the unoriginally named Route 66 Hotel, with an airplane parked out front, but I had already decided on the hotel I wanted to stay at—a Route 66 classic called the Blue Swallow Motel, which boasted one of the most recognized road signs on the Route.

Tucumcari was a curious town. It was like it had never gotten the memo that 66 had died. Nor had its myriad visitors. On the way to the hotel I had passed the La Cita Mexican restaurant, another well-known Route attraction. I checked into my room, then abandoned my pack and walked back to the restaurant.

La Cita was an L-shaped baby-blue structure with a twelve-foot plaster sombrero towering above its entry. My waitress was as authentically Mexican as the food.

I ordered chili relleno New Mexico–style, Caldo de Pecado—a fish soup—and fried ice cream. I suspect it's as difficult to get bad Mexican food in New Mexico as it is in Mexico. I walked back to the Blue Swallow and fell asleep on top of the bed.

The next three days I walked through Montoya (walking through town, all I could think of were the lines from *The Princess Bride*: *Hello. My name is Inigo Montoya. You killed my father. Prepare to die*), Newkirk, and Cuerro, finally ending up in Santa Rosa, an attractive little town with all the amenities of home. The original Route 66 went right through the town, which proudly claimed its heritage.

I rented a room at the Comfort Inn, then ate dinner at a Mexican restaurant called the Silver Moon.

Chapter Seven

Today I passed a turnoff to Las Vegas. I've lost more in Vegas than, perhaps, any man alive. And my loss had nothing to do with a roulette wheel or a deck of cards.

CHARLES JAMES'S DIARY

I ate breakfast at the hotel, then walked over to the Route 66 Auto Museum, advertised by a hot rod raised on a pole out in front of the building. Vintage cars were on display in the parking lot as well as inside. The restorations were all nicely done, except I couldn't figure out why someone would convert an Edsel into a tractor.

At its core, Route 66 culture has always been about cars, from the Okie jalopies of Steinbeck's Mother Road to the classic Corvette of the eponymous TV series.

I spent just an hour at the museum, since I was anxious to get back to my journey. I went back to the hotel and retrieved my pack, then started walking.

The road took me down a large hill, passing neon signs,

motels, and restaurants, then across the Pecos River, where Route 66 became 40 again. Parts of 66 still remained, which I walked when possible, but they were in pretty bad shape, mostly overgrown with weeds.

Twenty miles into the day I passed a sign designating the turnoff to Las Vegas. Las Vegas. That's where I was when Monica gave me back her wedding ring and pronounced the four words I'll never forget: "I'm not your pearl." Just seeing the sign brought pain. There was so much I would do differently. I read somewhere that too often what we want most in life is just the chance to do what we should have done to begin with. I could relate to that.

The road was barren, and I slept that night under an overpass.

The next morning around ten o'clock I came to the Milagro Food Mart, where I got something to eat and loaded up with several gallons of water, because I was told there wouldn't be any for a long way.

The New Mexico overpasses are all beautifully rendered with southwestern designs. It was a beautiful day and good walking, except for the weight of water.

Around noon I encountered my first sign for the Flying C Ranch:

YER GETTIN THERE.

Those three words marked the beginning of an onslaught of freeway signage—a southwestern version of Wall Drug's billboard advertising.

I passed signs offering:

INDIAN-MADE BLANKETS

CROSSES

SOUTHWEST JEWELRY

ROSE OPAL JEWELRY

MEXICAN IMPORTS

FIREWORKS

DAIRY QUEEN

MOCCASINS (AWESOME SELECTION!)

KID STUFF

AGATE BOOKENDS

SNAKE STUFF

KNIVES

MOTHER ROAD SOUVENIRS

CHICKEN SANDWICHES

POTTERY

SWEET TREATS

GUY STUFF

GIRL STUFF

And, just to make sure they'd covered their bases:

COOL STUFF

The myriad billboards covered both sides of the road, spaced only about fifty yards apart.

It was late afternoon when I reached the Flying C Ranch. As I waited in line to purchase some jerky, I listened to an elderly black man telling the man at the counter about his plans for retirement.

"I'm going to sleep in every day until one, then go to car shows and watch *Andy Griffith*. That's it. That's all I'm going to do."

The man at the counter replied, "What your old lady think of that?"

"She's not sure what to think," he said. "She's just upset that I'm going to be around all day."

I thought his plan sounded pretty great.

I ate dinner at the DQ inside the center, then camped out behind the building near a grove of mesquite trees.

The next morning I ate breakfast at the DQ—their country platter with bacon—then continued west on I-40, walking on old 66 whenever possible. There was nothing to see but billboards advertising the next big stop—Clines Corners. They had clearly copied Flying C, who had copied Wall Drug.

Clines Corners used to be a glitzy stop on 66, with an old western town. The street in front of Clines was called Yacht Club Drive, which was odd, for obvious reasons. I ate at the Clines Corner Café, then rented one of the trailer houses in back for the night.

Chapter Eight

Today I came across a man I thought was killing another man. He was trying to save his life. How poor our judgment is. Too often we open our eyes wide to condemn others.

CHARLES JAMES'S DIARY

The next three days were more of the same, though I did stop at two museums: the Glider Museum and the Antique Tractor and Toy Museum.

I passed through Wagon Wheel, Moriarty, Edgewood, and Barton, landing in the oddly named Zuzax. The town's name was made up by the enterprising owner of a curio shop hoping to attract attention.

I asked a man at the Zuzax campsite if I could put up my tent, and he told me that I could stay in a camper someone had abandoned. As I stepped into the tidy camper, I thought it was strange that someone would just pick up and leave. Then I remembered that it was what I had done, too.

The road out of Zuzax was a long, comfortable stretch of well-marked Route 66, which, subconsciously (or maybe consciously), was always reassuring to me.

After Zuzax came the town of Tijeras, which means *scissors* in Spanish. I walked along what they call the musical highway, which, if you're just walking, looks like one of those rumble strips they stamp into the side of the road to warn you that you've left your lane, but if you drive forty-five miles per hour, it plays "America the Beautiful." Fortunately, it was on the eastbound side of the road; otherwise I would have had to cross to the opposite side of the road, as people were driving on the edge of the road to hear it. I saw several cars turn around just to drive it again.

Just a couple of hours into the day, the town of Albuquerque appeared in the distance, spread out in the valley below me. I stopped and ate lunch at the Waffle House (it's always a good time to eat waffles), then followed Central into downtown Albuquerque. I passed a lot of old Route 66 businesses and signs intermingled with more modern designs. I was again reminded that public things are pretty in New Mexico—the medians and overpasses. Even the cars' license plates are brightly colored turquoise and yellow.

My pace slowed considerably, which is what happened whenever I entered a metropolitan area with its crowds and traffic signals.

I ate dinner at the famed Dog House, a small building with a neon sign of a dog wagging its tail and eating a string of hot dogs. The place was slammed, so I figured it must be good.

I ordered what their menu recommended—a chili dog

and a local delicacy called Frito pie. I chased it down with a Coke and a cherry shake.

After dinner I planned to walk until I found a place to spend the night, and I set out into the twilight.

As I approached the boulevard I noticed some violent activity across the street from me—a fight between two homeless men. The larger of the two men, who wore a cowboy hat, was crouched over the other, who lay motionless on his back. He was relentlessly beating him. My thought was that he would kill him if someone didn't intervene. I ran toward him, shouting, but he didn't stop. My heart began pounding wildly, anticipating the confrontation.

As I got closer I realized my mistake. The man on top wasn't beating him but was administering CPR. Homeless people were gathered around him, some looking concerned, others just curious.

When I got to the men I said, "Can I help?"

The cowboy glanced up at me. His forehead was wet with sweat, and it was obvious that he was exhausted from his efforts. "Do you know CPR?" he panted.

"Yes," I said. "I'm trained."

"I could use some help."

I kneeled down next to the prone man, who reeked. He probably hadn't bathed in months, if that. In addition, I think he must have soiled himself. I almost threw up, but fought to ignore it.

I put my hands on the prostrate man's chest and began giving compressions as the cowboy rolled back, groaning in exhaustion. "Thank you."

"Have you called 911?" I asked.

"They're on their way."

Almost immediately, I heard the sounds of approaching sirens.

"How long have you been at it?" I asked the cowboy.

"About ten minutes."

The man still showed no signs of life. A black-and-white patrol car was the first emergency vehicle to arrive on the scene. There were cars parked along the curb, so the police car was forced to park in the road. An officer got out of the car and walked up to us, sending several of the bystanders scurrying away.

He recognized the man in the cowboy hat.

"Hey, Eric. Crime scene?"

The cowboy shook his head. "No. I think he's had a heart attack."

The cop looked at me. "You certified in CPR?"

"Yes."

"Continue," he said, as if I had been awaiting his permission. The cop was clearly more interested in discovering whether a crime had been committed than providing assistance, which was fine, since just moments later an ambulance arrived at the scene with its lights and siren on, pulling up directly behind the police car.

The sirens stopped but the flashing emergency lights continued, bathing us in red-and-blue syncopated strobes. The ambulance door swung open, and I could hear a voice speaking on a radio: "Dispatch Rescue 44 has arrived on scene." Another voice returned, "Copy Rescue 44 at eighteen-oh-eight."

The two paramedics, both stocky, strong-looking men, erupted from the ambulance and into action. The first ran to us carrying several bags. "I'll take over," he said when he got to me. I leaned back away from the body, exhausted.

The paramedic rubbed his knuckles over the man's sternum and said, "Sir, can you hear me?" The man remained motionless. "No response; starting compressions."

The other paramedic, who had settled in across from us, started attaching wired, adhesive patches to the unconscious man's shoulders and the left lower side of his chest, followed by a blood pressure cuff and a monitor on his finger. Then he strapped a hard collar around his neck. He began pumping a bag over the man's mouth.

Another siren blared as a fire truck drove up behind the ambulance. Three men got out of the fire truck. One of the men was holding a stack of bright orange traffic cones. He walked behind the emergency vehicles and laid down the cones, merging the traffic into a single lane. He was joined by the police officer, who walked out into the street in front of the fireman to direct traffic away from him.

The first paramedic continued giving compressions, occasionally pausing for the other to give breaths with the bag mask.

Suddenly the second paramedic leaned over and vomited. The first paramedic just said, "He's pretty rank."

The paramedic wiped his mouth with his sleeve and continued. A moment later he said, "We've got a shockable rhythm. Continue compressions while I prepare for shock." He dialed up something on the monitor next to him, and it let out a high-pitched tone.

"Shock is ready; stop CPR and stand clear . . . delivering shock."

He pressed a button and the man's body jumped. "Resume CPR," he said.

A third man, from the fire truck, came over. "Got anything?" he asked.

"No, sir," the first paramedic said.

He crouched down next to the other men. "I'm going to insert," he said, reaching into one of the bags. He inserted an IV into the man's arm. "IV is in the right AC. I'm giving a first round of epi now."

There was another fireman near us writing on a pad and asking questions of the bystanders. The traffic in the street crawled as drivers rubbernecked to see what was happening.

"It's the oh-my-God squad," the second paramedic mumbled. "Freakin' vultures."

Suddenly the homeless man began vomiting, part of the expulsion landing on the paramedic's hands. (I considered this a good thing, since it was the only movement I'd seen from the man since I'd arrived.) The paramedic pulled off the mask and began suctioning up the vomit with a tube.

"What a waste of taxpayer dollars," I heard someone say. I looked over to see a man walking by on the sidewalk, his face twisted in hate. "Why do I even buy insurance?"

Sickeningly, I recognized the ugliness of his thoughts as once being my own. Several years ago, on an especially cold winter night in Detroit, we had a homeless guy come inside and fall asleep in the lobby outside my presentation.

I was furious when I saw him. "Drag that ugly carcass out of here," I told my staff.

"It's subzero outside," someone said.

"Then stay out with him and keep him warm with your bleeding heart." The remembrance of my insensitivity made my heart and stomach hurt.

The rescue attempt continued for what seemed at least five more minutes, until the fire captain said, "Let's transport."

One of the firemen opened the back doors of the ambulance and pulled out the stretcher along with a backboard, bringing them up next to the patient. The captain kept the man's head aligned with the body, while the second paramedic placed the backboard against the homeless man's back, then shouted, "On my count, roll him back!"

They rolled the man and the backboard together onto the ground. Remarkably, the first paramedic continued to administer CPR through all of it.

Then the men lifted him onto the stretcher. The second paramedic and the captain strapped the seat belts over the patient, securing him to the stretcher, and rolled the stretcher to the back doors of the ambulance and slid it inside, locking it into place.

The captain lifted a handheld radio from his utility belt and said, "Lovelace, this is Rescue 44. We have a fifty-year-old male found unresponsive on the sidewalk in full arrest. We have been performing CPR for approximately ten minutes with one shock delivered and a round of epi and a round of lidocaine. We're ready to administer another round of epi. The patient has unknown medications with unknown allergies. Any questions or orders at this time?"

"Negative," came the response. "We'll prepare for your arrival."

The first paramedic climbed into the back of the ambulance. The police car drove out first, leading the other two vehicles forward and then out into the intersection.

Even with the man gone, I could smell the stink on myself. It was nauseating. I turned and looked at the cowboy, who was lifting a canvas backpack from the ground. I guessed it belonged to the homeless man.

"Did you know him?" I asked.

He adjusted his hat. "Cliff." He looked at me. "His name was Cliff."

"He was a friend of yours?"

"They all are," he said.

"They?"

"These men," he said. "I run a shelter for men." He looked me over, then asked, "What's your name?"

"Charles James."

"What's your last name?"

"James is my last name."

"Like the outlaw."

"We're related."

"I guess that's cool. I'm Eric." He sniffed, then said, "Can't quite figure you out. You're articulate. Clean. But got the pack. Are you homeless?"

"For now," I said, amused by his observations.

"Well, if you need a place to stay, I have a shelter a couple of blocks from here."

I still don't know why, but I accepted his invitation. "If you have the room."

"I've got room. Come with me."

With the man's bag in hand, he turned and walked west down the sidewalk, stopping a few times to talk to the men we passed on the way. It was clear he had a rapport with them.

I followed him about two blocks to a large, yellow-bricked warehouse. We entered from a stairway that climbed halfway up the building to a second-story metal grate landing with an industrial door that had a thin slit of a window embedded with chicken wire.

The door opened to a small lobby with a semi-enclosed reception area. Past the lobby was a dim labyrinth of narrow hallways with men lining most of them.

Eric led me to his office, where he took his hat off and hung it on small deer antlers mounted on the wall. Then he sat down. "I'll just be just a moment. I've got to sign some papers."

I set my pack down on the vacant chair next to me. Eric started going through some papers when a short, husky man walked in. He glanced over at me and then said, "Sorry to bother you, sir."

Eric looked up. "What's up, Snoob?"

"Could I get the key to the cleaning closet?"

"What did you do with yours?"

"Lost it."

Eric shook his head and sighed. "Here. Bring it back this time. I mean it."

"Sorry, boss." He walked away.

"His name is Snoob?"

"That's his street name." He went back to his paperwork. "They all have street names."

"Like what?"

"Whatever. Viper. Cheddar. Shorty. Had a guy called Greyhound. He was a tall, slender fellow with gray hair."

"Why street names?"

He looked up at me. "I don't know that I could really tell you. Maybe disassociation."

"From the world?"

"From themselves, mostly. It's like this: not many people picture themselves as ever being homeless. They say that one in three Americans are one paycheck away from homelessness, but it's like death: we live in self-deceit. It's something that happens to other people.

"Fortunately, most people have family or friends. Safety nets. But not all. When people suddenly find themselves on the street, they feel like strangers from themselves. Add the fear and sleep deprivation, and pretty soon they don't know who they are anymore. They disassociate this new person from who they once were. Sometimes they have to treat themselves like a third person just to handle the shame." He looked back down, signed a few more papers, and then pushed them aside. "All right, that's done. I'll give you the tour."

"Should I bring my pack?"

"No. I'll lock the door."

We stepped out of his office. Eric locked the door behind us, then turned out toward a chair-filled room with a small dais and a microphone. There was a large television with at least a dozen men watching.

"This is our gathering room," he said. We turned a corner and stopped in front of a floor-to-ceiling grate. "My knee has been bothering me," he said. "We'll take the elevator." He looked down through the grate to where a man was loading boxes onto the flat industrial lift. "Clarence, can you give us a ride?"

A muscular thirtysomething-year-old man looked up at us from the floor below. "No problem, boss. Give me a second."

Clarence carried in another box, then stepped inside and pulled a lever. The elevator rose to our level and Eric lifted the grate. The elevator was mostly filled with boxes of clothing.

"How's it going?" Eric asked.

"Good," Clarence replied. "Got a big shipment of clothes in today."

"That's always good," Eric said.

"Watch your arm," Clarence said to me as he pulled the grate back down.

We stopped on the next floor, and Eric lifted the grate. "Our first stop is the bedroom. This is where you'll stay tonight."

We stepped off the elevator into a spacious, open room filled with bunk beds and divided by wooden supports that rose like trees every twenty feet or so. The walls of the room were painted brick, though the paint looked as aged as everything else in the building.

There were three large windows on the far end of the room covered with red fabric curtains, glowing from the setting sun. Fluorescent lights hung from the ceiling in rows of three.

I figured that there were at least thirty of the pipe-framed bunk beds, spaced about a yard apart from one another. The bedding was eclectic, everything from stained white sheets to SpongeBob SquarePants prints.

There were a few men in the room already sleeping. The place smelled of body odor, tobacco, and urine. Not unbearably bad, but enough to be unpleasant—like talking to somebody with bad breath.

Eric looked at me and said, "I know, the smell takes some getting used to. We have a rule that if they spend the night, they have to shower."

"They don't all spend the night?"

"No. Some prefer the street. And it's Albuquerque, so they're not going to freeze to death. Some just come by for a little help. We have what we call the Shower and Shave Day. Every Monday, Wednesday, and Friday anyone can come in for a shower and shave. After they shower we let them look through our clothes and pick out something."

"Where do you get your clothes?"

"Donations. Churches. Clothing drives."

"You've got a lot of beds."

"Fifty-six," he said. "We use them all. If it gets cold, we can also lay pads out in the rec room.

"Over here," he continued, leading me around the corner, "is the locker and clothing room." The room had a Dutch door, the bottom half shut and the top half opened back into the room. Eric opened the bottom part of the door and we stepped into a rectangular room crowded with boxes and clothing.

One side of the room was covered with plastic milk crates that were turned on their sides and stacked from floor to ceiling. The rest of the room was filled with miscellaneous clothing racks. Cardboard boxes were stacked two deep against the walls.

Standing behind the row of crates was a young man about my height, covered with tattoos. A curly tuft of tan hair escaped his beanie. He wore a T-shirt and sweat pants. He was folding clothes and setting them in piles.

"What are all these boxes?" Eric asked.

"Big haul, man. Someone dropped off a truckload this morning. Great stuff. All new clothes. Still got the tags on them."

Eric looked around at the boxes and said, "Well, cut them off."

"Will do, boss."

Before I could ask, Eric said, "If we leave the tags on them, they'll just sell them. Fund their addictions." He looked through one of the boxes and lifted out a pair of ski goggles. "Derrick will like this. He snowboards."

"Nice," the young man said.

"Do the men have to contribute to stay?"

"By contribute, you mean work?" I nodded. "No. But we encourage them to help. It's good for them. Serving others brings about a change in their souls. It gives them purpose. They start feeling good about themselves again."

"They must love you."

"Some do. Some don't feel much gratitude about anything. I've been punched, spit on. It's like they say, no good deed goes unpunished."

"How do you take that?"

"I found Christ. Or he found me." Eric turned back to the room. "This little locker room right here may not seem like much, but it's more important than you can imagine. One of the big problems the homeless face is sleep deprivation. Sleeping outdoors, they're always worried about their things being stolen. Of course, it's not just that. They live in fear of being attacked or robbed or raped. Or even being harassed by police. It's a crime in most cities to sleep in a public place. They learn to sleep with one eye open."

"Someone's always here watching their things?"

"If not, it's locked."

The room was attached to a smaller room that was also filled with clothing, some on racks, others on shelves marked with sizes. There was a serving window that opened onto the main bedroom. The window had a metal awning that could be pulled down and locked.

"This is our distribution room. They can get a razor and soap and shampoo. Then, after they shower, they can choose new clothes."

"Old wine in new bottles," I said.

He grinned. "Exactly."

I followed him around to the bathroom, which had four toilets next to each other. "Not much privacy," I said.

"Privacy's not a good thing in a place like this." He stepped over to an opening that had a long row of showers. "This is new. Six showers. The men who stay here are required to shower each day. It keeps the smell tolerable and helps our beds last longer. Some of these people coming in haven't showered for a while. One guy told me he hadn't showered for more than four years."

We walked through a back door that led us down a narrow corridor back to the elevator. "I'll show you the pantry."

The elevator took us to the bottom level. It opened onto a concrete-walled basement. The concrete was bare and cracking, with large chunks missing in places. An American flag was hung on the wall above a set of barbells and a bench-press machine. To the side of the room was the gunmetal-gray door of a walk-in refrigerator.

"This is our refrigerator," he said. "This space also doubles as our workout room. It's mostly used by the guys going through recovery." I followed him to the next room. "This is our food pantry."

A powerful-looking man glanced up from a chair near the door. "Hey, Sundance. Where's your hat?"

"I left it upstairs."

"Almost didn't recognize you. Who's this guy?"

"Charles," I said.

"I'm Charles, too," he said. "Great names."

As we walked away, I turned to Eric. "Sundance?"

"As in the Sundance Kid."

"That's your street name?"

"It's the one they gave me."

"Because of your hat?"

"Because I'm a quick draw," he said.

I followed him down an aisle of heavy wood and metal

shelves. The food they stored was eclectic. Protein bars, Hostess pies, cans of Crisco, mac and cheese, pasta, generic peanut butter, and taco shells.

"Where do you get the food?"

"Donations. Everything here is donated. We have a few grocery stores that send us things daily. Day-olds from their bakery, but a lot more than that, too. Dented cans, food that's technically expired but still good, produce on its last legs. We've got some restaurants, too. And there are always a few church groups who will do food drives.

"We've got a downtown church that's really good to us. That's where we get our things for our Sunday breakfasts. Every Sunday morning we go out and set up under the viaduct and feed about five hundred people."

"Sunday? Tomorrow morning?"

"Yes. You're welcome to help. We can always use it."

"I'd be glad to."

He turned back to the shelves. "So the pantry is our first line of defense for the homeless. Obviously, it's better to keep people in homes than to deal with them on the streets. I know that's common sense, but common sense isn't always that common.

"Sometimes people face a demon's dilemma. They have to make a choice between buying food or paying the rent. Of course they're going to buy food. But if we can get them food, they pay their rent and don't end up homeless. Which also means they don't lose their jobs and end up needing shelter and food as well. It's first-level intervention—it's always better to build a fence on top of the cliff than to put an ambulance at the bottom of it. Cheaper, too."

"I've used that in my speeches," I said.

"Speeches?" he said.

"My past life," I said.

He shrugged, accepting my simplified answer. "Well, it's just common sense."

We stepped out of the pantry into a hallway.

"Do you ever have problems here?" I asked.

"There are always problems here. What do you mean, specifically?"

"Violence."

"Fighting," he said. "It happens. Not as much as you think, but it happens."

"How do you keep it down?"

"Most of these men are no more violent than you and me. The difference is they don't often get to choose their company. Add stress, fear, and anger to that, and I'm surprised there's not a lot more. But we let them know that any violence will get them kicked out of here. Both the puncher and the punched."

"The punched? That doesn't seem fair."

"Thing is, unless they're drunk, no one goes around throwing indiscriminate punches. If you get punched, nine out of ten times you were doing something to provoke it. I say, you throw gas on the fire, it's your own fault if you get burned."

"Still seems harsh."

"Harsh or not, it works. I haven't had to throw anyone out for more than a year. For the most part, they watch out for each other. Like family."

"You're saying there's a family atmosphere here?"

He smiled. "Yeah, it's a family all right. But it's a big ol' dysfunctional one. They'll do what they can to take care of each other, but if they get the chance, they'll steal from each other, too."

"How many of these men have mental illnesses?"

"Not many. I know there's a lot on the street, but we don't take them. We're not equipped for it. So when someone comes in, we try to get them help. But you can't force them to get help, and they're so suspicious or afraid of the police and society that they usually won't take it. So we do our best to get them off drugs and on real medications. Otherwise we just send them on their way."

We came to the end of the corridor, which opened into a large, industrial kitchen with stainless-steel appliances and counters. There were three men inside, preparing food. One was frying hamburgers on a wide grill, and the other two were chopping vegetables. They were all wearing aprons and beanie caps. They looked over at us as we entered.

"Hey, y'all," the griller said. "Look sharp. Boss is here."

"Hey, Marky," Eric said. He turned to me. "This is our kitchen, obviously. We run two shifts a day. The menu depends on what we get. But breakfast pretty much stays the same: eggs, pancakes, potatoes, and whatever meat we can wrangle. The rest is potluck."

We walked into the adjacent room. Plastic chairs were

stacked in rows a dozen high. The tables were the kind that folded up from the middle. The floor was white and black linoleum squares. "This is the dining area."

"How many people do you feed a day?"

"Close to a hundred." He breathed out. "That's it; let's go back and get your pack."

We walked back to his office. He unlocked the door and we both walked inside. Eric sat down at his desk.

"May I ask you something?" I said.

He looked back up at me.

"How did you get into all this?"

"Wasn't exactly something I was expecting from life. But life's never the picture we think we're painting.

"I was just living, you know. I thought I was a pretty good guy, going to church every Sunday, praying, paying tithing, even sang in the choir. Then God threw a monkey wrench into the cogs of my piety. I had an older brother who was bipolar."

I noticed his use of the past tense.

"As he got older, it got worse. He ended up homeless."

"Aren't there medications to help manage that?"

"Yes, but they only work if you take them. In some ways, the disease is its own seduction. When you're down, you don't care enough about yourself to help yourself, and when you're on a manic high, you don't want help. You're on top of the world." He shrugged. "Why would you take a drug to make you feel bad?

"When he had manic episodes, he believed he was wealthy—really wealthy, like Jeff Bezos and Warren Buffett combined. He'd buy new cars he couldn't afford, expensive gifts for friends. There were always salespeople ready to relieve him of his money. Or credit. Once he bought me a Rolex watch. One of those President ones, with a pearl face and diamond-ringed bezel. I tried to give it back, but he said if I did, he'd take it as an insult and flush it down the toilet. He wasn't joking. He would have.

"He eventually broke with reality and was fired from his job. Not long after that, his wife left him. She got the house and he moved into an apartment, but he didn't keep up the payments and lost it. He started roaming from state to state. Every now and then I'd get a call from him. He was always in some new city, sleeping in his car. Then he lost his car. Then his phone. I had no idea where he was. He ended up in northern Utah. They have hard winters there."

"I was raised in northern Utah," I said.

"Then you know." His demeanor turned softer. "Police found him under an overpass on Christmas Day. He died from exposure."

"I'm sorry," I said.

"It changed everything for me. That's when I decided to go in a different direction. I started volunteering with the homeless. I found a church that fed them every Sunday under a viaduct. Eventually I took it over.

"Then I found this place. It was abandoned, and people were squatting in it. I went to the owner and worked out a deal. We'd keep it clean, lower his liability, and give him enough to pay the taxes. Good for everybody." He frowned. "It was good while it lasted. Nothing lasts forever, right?"

"What do you mean?"

He shook his head. "I don't know why my tongue is so loose with you. The owner just put the building up for sale. We're being evicted."

"Where will you go?"

He shrugged. "We don't have anyplace to go. We've been running on fumes for the last two years." He shook his head. "The thing is, the crisis is just getting worse. I feel like I'm trying to put out a house fire with a thimbleful of water."

I looked at him for a moment, then said, "Can I help?"

"You wouldn't have an extra million in your back pocket, would you? Heck, I'd take fifty grand."

Before I could say anything, he said, "It is what it is. I'll be serving breakfast in the morning if you want to help."

"Where and when?"

"We start at six. It's just a few blocks from here. Due west under the overpass."

"I'll be there." I picked up my pack to go.

"Hey, thanks for your help today out there on the street."

"You're welcome. Do you think he'll make it?"

"No." He breathed out slowly. "I'll see you in the morning. Sleep well."

"Thank you," I said. "You, too."

I walked out through a cluster of men to the stairway and climbed to the top floor of the building, coming out near the elevator. This time the bedroom was crowded. I looked around, not sure how to claim a bed. One of the men standing near the clothes dispensary said, "First time?"

"Yeah."

"You've got to shower."

"I showered this morning."

"No exceptions," he said. "Everyone showers."

"All right." I looked around. "Can I take any bed?"

"After you shower, yeah. Unless someone's in it."

I chose a bed near the far wall and lay my shirt across it. Many of the men were walking around in their underwear, so I stripped down to my briefs, then went to the locker room to check my pack.

"Need a towel?" the man in the locker room asked.

"Yes."

"Here you go." He handed me a worn terry cloth towel embroidered with the name of a local Marriott. I took my place in the line of men outside the bathroom. Most of them were naked, though a few had towels wrapped around them. The line moved steadily in single file toward the narrow bathroom entry.

When I reached the outer bathroom I saw several men sitting on toilets, all of them nude, talking. I envied them for feeling so at ease in their own skin. Vanity is the first casualty of poverty.

It took only five minutes to reach the shower, faster than I anticipated. Apparently, they didn't care much for long showers. The bathroom had six narrow showers with a tile wall between them but no door or curtain. The tile leading to the showers was streaked with mud.

I took the first shower available, one of the middle ones. There was still dirt on the floor from the last bather.

Or maybe a string of them—old dirt these guys had carried around for a while. I guess all dirt is old.

In my previous life it would have been humiliating, walking around in a strange place, buck naked with a crowd of men whom most people would cross the sidewalk for on the street, but it just was what it was. No one else seemed to mind the experience, other than objecting to the water itself.

I took a quick shower, dried myself off, and then put on my underwear. As I walked out of the bathroom, the locker guy said, "Leave the towel in the box."

I wiped my neck and underarms again, then threw down my towel. I walked back over to the bed I had claimed, glad to see that it was still vacant. I put on my shirt and pulled down the dark-blue sheet, making sure there was nothing crawling around inside. Then I lay down.

Across from me on the lower bunk a man was lying on his back reading a Louis L'Amour novel. He glanced over at me and then sat up and leaned forward, extending his hand across the space between our bunks. "I'm Justin."

He looked like a weathered, thinner version of Mark Wahlberg with long sideburns. He wore Levi's and a grayish-blue long-sleeved shirt with its sleeves rolled up to just below his elbow. He had a three-inch scar across one of his cheeks, which was partially concealed by whiskers.

"Charles," I said.

"Nice to meet you, Charles. First night here?"

"Yes. How can you tell?"

"I haven't seen you before."

That made sense. "I'm just passing through town."

"Gotcha," he said. "Where you from?"

"Chicago."

"Windy City. Where you headed?"

"California."

"Nice place," he said. "A lot warmer than Chicago. I like the northern part. Monterey Bay. I served up there for a time in the Presidio."

"You were in the military?"

"I did four tours in Afghanistan."

"How did you end up here?"

"That's a story," he said. Coming back is . . . it's just crazy. Have you ever walked out of a theater into the real world and felt disoriented? It's like that on steroids. It's like, even with the insanity of war, things made more sense in Afghanistan. I knew what I was supposed to do. I had a purpose. I had friends to do it with."

"Why didn't you stay?"

"Wasn't my choice. I was discharged for medical reasons. We were out on a patrolling mission when we hit an IED. It killed my team." He frowned. "I had the bad luck to survive.

"The blast took off my foot. I was in the hospital for a few weeks. But the worst part was that something about my brain just felt wrong. That's what the army shrinks decided, too. They gave me a discharge and sent me home.

"I fought it. I mean, I was glad to be back with my

wife, at least until I found out that she was stepping out on me. She was cheating with some big-toothed guy who owned a car dealership. He's on the Albuquerque TV all the time, talking about his honest deals.

"One day she came home beat up. I went nuts. I told her I was going to go kill the guy, so she called the police. When they got there, she told them I had beaten her up. They handcuffed me and took me to jail. Judge didn't believe a word I said. Said I was 'unrepentant' and sentenced me to three months in jail. When I got out, my wife had taken everything and filed a restraining order. Everything I had was gone."

"You had no one to help you?"

"No. Family's a mess. That's why I joined the army to begin with. I only had a few friends left from Afghanistan. While I was in jail they both committed suicide. Within two days of each other."

"I'm really sorry," I said.

"Yeah, me, too," he said. "I got a job at a warehouse, moving hoses around. But it was hard with my foot hurt. Then I kept blacking out. Something to do with my PTSD. That really freaked them out. When I lost my job, I had nothing but a few hundred bucks and the clothes on my back. I went to the army surplus store and bought me a tent. Found a place to set it up, then just spent my days wandering.

"A couple of weeks later I woke in the night to a bunch of shouting. My tent was collapsed around me like a big sack. There was a gang. I couldn't understand them; they were shouting things in Spanish, but they were kicking me. I was a prisoner in my tent, so I didn't know where the next hit was gonna come from, so I couldn't block anything. I just tried to curl up, you know, like a baby before it's born."

"Fetal position," I said.

"Yeah. One of 'em must have had a pipe or a baseball bat, something hard like that; whenever it came down it stunned me. That beating was worse than the IED, 'cause there was no meaning to it. And it just kept on going. I knew they were going to kill me. They broke my collarbone and more than half my ribs before something hit me in the head and I was out.

"I don't know how long I was out, but when I came to, I was lying outside the tent, bleeding. They'd taken everything I had. Even my shoes.

"I couldn't move for the longest time. I remember just lying there wiping blood off me and looking up as some guy walked by and said, 'Get a life.' Makes me think of the guy in the Bible, the one who gets beaten and robbed, the Sammon . . . Sammer . . ."

"The Samaritan," I said.

"Yeah. People just walked by me. Then this man in a cowboy hat walks up to me, takes a look at me, and says, 'Someone in there?'"

"Eric," I said.

"Yeah. He knelt down next to me and gave me his hand and said, 'C'mon, brother. Let's get you some help.' I had no idea who he was or what he wanted, but I wasn't exactly picky, you know? You're drowning and someone throws you a life ring, you don't ask where they got it.

"He took me into his car and gave me some water and a box of crackers, then drove me to the hospital. He waited there until the doctor saw me. I got to spend the night there. I was glad for that. Food and a clean bed. Nice people. A warm shower.

"The next day Eric came back for me. He even brought some shoes. He brought me here. I've been here ever since. I don't know what I'd do without him and this place."

I thought about what Eric had told me about shutting the place down. I guessed he hadn't told anyone yet.

"I help him run the food bank. He pays me a hundred dollars a week. I know it doesn't sound like much, but it's respectable, you know?"

I nodded. There were times when I had made that much in a second.

"I used to stand out there on the side of the road with a sign that said, 'Vet, can you help?' There was a guy at the freeway on-ramp just one down from me with a vet sign, too. He didn't look like a vet. You can smell someone who's seen combat, and this guy was a wanker.

"One day I asked him where he was deployed. He said, 'Iraq.' I said, 'What unit?' He just stared at me, then threw out some made-up, bull-puck number that meant nothing. I went off on him. He turned and ran. My friends died over there, and he's back here taking the credit. Stolen valor, you know? I chased after him. But I can't run fast anymore, not with just one foot. When I caught up to him, the skunk jumped into a BMW and drove off. Car still had the dealer plates. Lucky for him he never came back, or I might have beaten him to a pulp.

"They shouldn't have sent me home," he said, slowly shaking his head. "There's something about belonging to a tribe, you know? The other day I read something. When the colonists came from England, a lot of the white people just took off into the wild and joined up with the Indians. But none of the Indians joined the white people. Not one of them. When I heard that, I thought, wait a minute. The white people were supposed to have it better, right? They had better living conditions, more luxury things, more modern things. I mean, the Indians were basically still living in the Stone Age. But that's not what matters. The more affluent a society, the more depression there is. The more suicide. We just want to belong to something.

"It hasn't changed in two hundred years. People are more isolated today than ever. They don't even know their neighbors. Something's got to change."

I nodded slowly. "You're right."

Suddenly a call went out over the PA system. "Lights out, gentlemen."

"Must be ten," Justin said. "Well, I've bent your ear enough. I'll let you sleep."

"It's nice meeting you," I said.

"You, too, brother. Night."

"Night."

Judging from the sound of his breathing, he was asleep in less than five minutes.

I didn't sleep well. It was noisy. It sounded like a saw-mill. Mostly I just wasn't used to sleeping around so many people.

Or maybe it was knowing that they'd soon all be back out on the streets.

Chapter Nine

I'm ashamed to admit that I've spent more than a thousand dollars on a meal I didn't finish when there are many who count a full belly as a rarity and a hot meal as ecstasy.

CHARLES JAMES'S DIARY

I woke the next morning to snoring. The guy in the bunk above me sounded like a chain saw. Our bed vibrated. I looked at my watch. It was a quarter to seven, which meant I had missed Eric. I got up and got my backpack, then walked out into the cool, moist air and headed west.

It was still dark as I walked under the viaduct. There was a flat, open patch of pavement beneath the bridge with several men walking around. Eric was there, the silhouette of him in his cowboy hat cutting an easily recognizable figure. He was standing before a dozen or more people on the back of an open trailer, its door lowered to the ground, creating a ramp.

Eric nodded at me, then started speaking in a tone that sounded like a memorized speech.

"Listen up, compadres. My name is Eric, and you're in my show. That makes you my stagehands. I've been doing this for thirteen years. You've been here for all of thirteen minutes. If you just do what I say, things go smoothly. You want to do it your way, go find Sinatra and the two of you can sing about it. You all good with that?"

There were shrugs and nods of submission.

"Good. Then we'll get along well enough and get some people fed. Thank you all for coming. Even those of you who don't want to be here." He put his arm around a skinny young Hispanic man. "This is Jedediah; we call him Jed." He pointed at some of the men who were standing to the side. "You six right here do what Jed says. Whether it's from his mouth or mine, it's all the same."

"All right," Jed said, trying to sound bigger than he was. "Let's move these tables. We're going to make a perimeter." He made it sound more like a setup for war than breakfast.

Peculiarly, pigeons began flying down even before we had started bringing out the food. I suppose that they knew what we were up to.

"James," Eric said. "Come up here and help me with the stoves."

I walked up the ramp to the back of the trailer. We carried out two propane stoves to the east perimeter of the tables. Eric crouched down and began attaching the rubber hoses from the stoves to the wide-lipped mouths of the propane tanks. I watched him for a moment, then asked, "Why would anyone be here if they didn't want to be?"

He looked up at me. "What?"

"You said, 'Even those of you who don't want to be here.' If they don't want to be here, why would they be here?"

He went back to screwing the valve onto the tank. "Court-ordered community service. You're surrounded by miscreants and scofflaws."

We finished setting up the stoves and lit them. Then Eric led me to the center of the area where food and coffee were being prepared. In the course of our walk he suddenly stopped and shouted at a man who was stirring eggs in a bowl. "No, no, no! We'll all starve if you do it like that. You don't stir the eggs, you beat them like a naughty child."

"That's what got me in jail," the man said.

"Save it for the judge. I want to hear the spoon clanking against the sides."

We walked up to a table where a tall, abnormally thin man with tangled black hair and thick Buddy Holly glasses was laying out bowls.

"Put these on," Eric said, handing me a pair of latex gloves. "I'm putting you in charge of pancake production.

"This is Garrett. He'll show you the ropes. If you need anything, I'm out front." He walked away, leaving me with the odd-looking man.

Garrett turned to me. "What's your name?"

"Charles," I said.

"I heard Eric call you James."

Then why did you ask? I thought. "That's my last name."

Garrett looked at me as if what I'd said was beyond his comprehension.

"I don't care either way," I said. "Call me whatever you want."

"Charles, then," he decided. "Have you made pancakes before?"

"Everyone's made pancakes."

"Doesn't matter what you think you know," he said. "We've got a system for it."

I was starting to get annoyed at how intense everyone was around here. We were making breakfast, not munitions.

Garrett pulled out a white plastic bucket and pried off its lid. "This is pancake mix." He took a plastic cup from the table. "You got your cup. You take twelve cups. Twelve. Hours on a clock. Count them out loud or else you'll forget."

"I won't forget."

"You'll forget. Just listen. We've got a system. You don't want to throw off the system."

After we had mixed the batter, we poured it into plastic pitchers, then carried them over to a table next to one of the stoves Eric and I had set up. Its surface was now smoking. A massive can of Crisco sat on a lipped cookie sheet.

Garrett spooned a quarter cup of Crisco onto a paper towel, then ran it across the grill until it was covered in grease. He grabbed the first plastic pitcher, lifting it by its handle over to the grill. "Dip the spoon in the pitcher, lift out a heaping spoonful, and drop it on the grill. Eight pancakes per line, three lines. That's eight times three, twenty-four coaster-sized hotcakes. You got it?"

"Got it," I said. "You've got a system."

"Darn tootin'." He stood over the grill. "The grill's hot. That's good, because it means you can cook faster. But you got to be careful. Eric doesn't like blondes. And you'll hear it."

"That's a non sequitur," I said.

"What's a non sequitur?"

"You said Eric doesn't like blondes. Does he like redheads?"

"I'm not talking about the female species," he said. "I'm talking about the internal consistency of the cakes. You got blondes and brunettes. Eric likes brunettes. Brunettes don't have gooey interiors." He scooped the pancakes up, putting them in an aluminum cake pan. "After each batch you scrape off the grill, put on more grease, and start over. Now you do it."

I went for the pancake mix.

"The Crisco!" he shouted. "Crisco first. Follow the system."

"Right," I said. "Sorry."

I began spooning on the cakes. I don't know why he didn't just pour it. It would have been easier.

"I said *heaping* spoonfuls!"

After I had filled the grill, he said, "Okay, while the first side is cooking, we take the last batch of cakes over to the warming trays."

I followed him over to the first table, where there were aluminum warming trays filled with food. It's also where the homeless were lined up to be served.

Garrett lifted the lid off the cakes and set them inside in careful rows. Then he replaced the lid sideways, leaving an opening in the trays. "When you're done, don't put the lid on tight or it will rain condensation on the cakes."

"No rain," I said.

"No rain," he repeated. "Now we head back to the grill. The ones you put on should be ready to flip. You'll get the rhythm of it."

I went back to my pancakes. As I was turning them over, I asked Garrett, "What do you do when you're not flipping pancakes?"

"I fix clocks."

"Does anyone still have a clock?"

"It's a niche," he said.

At least it explained the overly precise way he counted and measured everything.

Eric's voice boomed over a loudspeaker. "Welcome. We're glad you're here. Before we eat, I will praise God." He bowed his head. "Dear God, we are here to partake of food and praise Thee. Thank you for our bounty. Amen."

Only a few of the people said amen.

"All right. Let's have plates one to fifteen. One to fifteen."

"The plates are numbered?" I asked.

"There's a system," Garrett said.

"Of course there is," I said.

"There's a reason for everything."

After another cycle of pancakes, Garrett nodded at me, as if he were proud of his student. Or, more likely, proud of his mentorship. Under his tutelage it was difficult to remember that these were just pancakes.

"I've taught you well," he said. "I'll leave you now."

I half-expected him to say, "Now bow to your sensei." (For the record, I wouldn't have.) I didn't ask him where he was going. I didn't care. I was just glad he was gone.

I went through a few more cycles—grease, spoon, deliver, flip, stack, repeat—when a woman began yelling at Eric. She was just a few feet from him and screaming, to the point that saliva was flying from her mouth. I couldn't tell from her rambling what she was upset about. Amazingly, Eric just looked at her, as calm as the pigeons around us. It took a few minutes before the woman settled herself down.

About half an hour later, after I had filled all the warming trays, Eric walked up to me. "Have you eaten yet?"

"No."

"Take a break. Get something to eat. It's good for them to see us eat."

"So they know it's edible?"

"So they know we don't think we're better than them."

I walked up to the food warmers. Next to the containers I had filled with pancakes was one with scrambled eggs, mashed potatoes, and white sawmill gravy. The man serving the food dropped a pile of mashed potatoes on my plate, then pressed them down with the back of his spoon, making a small crater.

"Eggs?" he asked.

"Yes, please."

He scooped a heaping spoon of eggs on my plate next

to the potatoes. Then he asked, "You want gravy on your eggs?" When I didn't answer he said, "You should, it's really good."

The homeless man in line next to me said, "Yeah. Really good." I looked at the man. He was missing most of his front teeth.

"Sure," I said.

The server ladled the white gravy over the pile of egg.

At the table next to the warming trays was a man with two large bottles, one filled with small yellow peppers, the other with large pickled jalapeños and carrots. I tried a carrot and it burned my mouth. The Hispanic man serving them laughed at me. "*Muy picante, no?*"

"*Muy*," I said.

Farther down the table were large trays of packaged cookies, then orange beverage holders, each marked with a piece of paper that was written on with marker and taped to the container.

Coffee
Cocoa
Sunny-D
Water

I got a coffee and then sat down on a concrete ledge. At least a dozen pigeons joined me, but none of the homeless people.

As I was finishing my meal, Eric came and sat next to me.

"How was your night?"

"My night was good. And this is amazing. It's quite a machine you've got going here. A well-wound clock."

"You've been around Garrett too long," he said. "Yeah, I'm hoping I can at least keep this going after we shut down the home. We've got the trailer paid for. That's what I sold my brother's Rolex for. The trailer, ovens, everything we needed."

"I bet you've seen some interesting things down here," I said.

He nodded. "Word."

"How did you get this place?"

"This viaduct? The city gave us a permit. I mean, look at it; they don't care."

I looked around. It was the first time I'd noticed that rising up next to us was a billboard with a picture of a Ferrari and a beautiful woman advertising an exotic car dealership. It just seemed ironic to me, like that famous Depression-era picture of people standing in a soup line in front of a car advertisement. I guess this was the contemporary version of that.

"Actually, it was almost tragic how I found this place."

"How is that?"

"Right up there," he said, pointing to a ledge, "one of my men was threatening to jump. He had run out of his medications and thought the government had planted a microphone in his neck."

"That's heartbreaking."

"What's heartbreaking is that people were actually encouraging him to do it. I saw a woman with two kids in the car shout at him to jump."

I shook my head. "What happened?"

"The police cut a hole in the fence, then I brought him some pizza and coaxed him back in. Got him to a hospital and got him on medications. You saw him yesterday. That was Marky. He was in the kitchen." He breathed out. "Rarely a dull day."

"So what has this taught you about society?"

He smiled. "No one has ever asked me that. I've got this theory," he said. "Back in history there was space. Physical space. Space has always been the issue. Manifest Destiny, the frontier, whatever you want to call it. Space to live. We need space.

"In the early days of our country, there were hermits and recluses and mountain men. People who didn't want to socialize with the ilk of the day, so they'd just come in to trade some pelts now and then and then go back out on their own. That doesn't exist now. There's no place to hide. The land is now all parceled and owned and leased."

"You're saying these people want to be here?"

"Of course not. But some of them do. I know this. I'm not being political, I'm being pragmatic. I know what I know. Some of these people could be given money and brought back into proper society and they'd be back here digging through Dumpsters the next week.

"Then some of them need help from society and don't get it. Some say it could be done with the churches, but they're not doing it. If one of my guys stumbled into some of the churches around here, they'd be ushered out.

"What they don't remember is that this, right here, is

a church. Right here under the bridge. People think of the Second Coming, like Jesus is going to meet up in a cathedral or temple, but if Jesus came here today, this is where he'd be. Under the viaduct. That's where he spent his life. He only went to the synagogues to give them the what-for. He spent his time with the shamed, the outcasts, the tax collectors. The pious drove him crazy. He didn't party with the Pharisees."

"Pharisees don't party," I said.

"Yeah. I suppose it's just as well."

"That woman shouting at you. What was that about?"

"She was high on something."

"But you still fed her."

He nodded. "'Course. She was hungry."

There was something remarkably noble about his answer. It reminded me of the waitress in Groom. When I asked her why she was helping me she said, "Because you needed help." As if it were the most obvious thing in the world.

"Some people just need help," Eric said, echoing my thoughts. "I had a man in the shelter a few years back. His name was Huang Nyguy. He was Vietnamese. His father was an American GI. I don't know if you know what it's like for those of mixed race in Vietnam, but they're complete outcasts. Treated worse than animals. So his father brings him to America. He has trouble learning English. To make it worse, he has seizures.

"Eventually Huang leaves home and gets a job at a Vietnamese restaurant. But he keeps having seizures. He can't make it. One day, the owner of the restaurant drives him here, drops him off out front of the shelter.

"I wasn't sure what to do with him. He just sat in the corner of our rec room for almost two weeks. I've never seen anyone looking more sad and hopeless in my life.

"Finally, I called the woman who brought him. I said, 'Tell me about him.' She says, 'Huang isn't like us. He needs someone to look over him.' That's when I realized that he was incapable of taking care of himself. I worked with the state, eventually got him into assisted living.

"I saw him last week. He was smiling. The woman there told me that everyone likes him. That he's very helpful and kind and always helping the elderly people." He looked at me. "I think I saved his life. If he'd been here much longer I'm sure he would have killed himself."

"Saint Sundance."

Eric frowned. "No, don't you go putting me on a pedestal. I keep close to the ground. It's a shorter fall."

I finished eating. "Time to clean up?" I asked.

"We're good," he said. "I've got lots of help today. You get back on the road. You've got a ways to go."

"Hope to see you again," I said. "Hang in there."

"You never know," he said. "Miracles happen. Maybe an angel will show up."

"You never know," I said. I grabbed my backpack. "See you later, cowboy."

"See you, outlaw."

I shrugged on my pack, then headed off down Route 66 and into the river of humanity.

Chapter Ten

I can walk away from Albuquerque, but what I experienced will follow me.

CHARLES JAMES'S DIARY

It was Sunday morning and the city was quiet. Even so, walking was choppy, with traffic lights at every corner. I ignored as many of the lights as I could.

Outside of Albuquerque there is a long stretch of gradual incline as the city fades. It's called Nine Mile Hill. I don't remember much more than that. My thoughts were preoccupied with my experiences of the previous two days. I couldn't get Eric or Justin or the shelter men off my mind. I had spent my professional life not only exhorting people to recklessly pursue their self-interest, but I had done so myself. Everything had been about me. Always the constant clamor of *me, me, me*. And the result was that I had been showered with wealth and luxury.

Then there was Eric, a man who took little or no thought for himself. A man who somehow had toppled the tyrant of self-interest and was not only living the life of a homeless man but also struggling to keep the shelter open. *Where's the justice in that?*

And then there was Justin. He had risked his life for a home and country that had betrayed him when he needed them most. What would happen to him if the shelter closed? What would happen to all of those men? Was there no one to help them? Why would a just God not intervene to help someone like that? Then it occurred to me. Maybe he just had.

A little after noon I passed a sign announcing the "End of Albuquerque." I left the highway for the frontage road, the Sandia Mountains rising ahead of me in the distance. By late afternoon I reached the historic Rio Puerco Bridge, a bypassed crossing that cars were no longer allowed on.

Across from the bridge was the Route 66 Hotel and Casino, announced by a massive neon outline of the Route 66 shield over the casino's entryway. I was still tired from my lack of sleep, so I decided to end my day a little early and spend the night.

The hotel wasn't crowded. I got a basic room, but compared to the shelter, it felt like a presidential suite. Einstein taught us that time is relative. But everything in life is.

I took a long shower, then went down to the casino's all-you-can-eat buffet. It was seafood night, and I ate my fill of crab and shrimp. I paid the extra nine dollars for a lobster tail. Buffets are excellent when you've been walking all day.

As I was leaving the restaurant I could hear a party

going on in the club. There was a time when I would have been drawn to the energy. Heck, there was a time when I was throwing that kind of party. Now, even as alone as I was, I felt repulsed by the shallowness of it all.

I went up to my room and went to bed.

Chapter Eleven

I don't think it odd that Hemingway may have written The Old Man and the Sea while landlocked out here in the desert. Our heads and our feet are rarely in the same room.

CHARLES JAMES'S DIARY

For the rest of the day I walked on Laguna Pueblo land. The landscape was beautiful. I walked past Owl Rock—named by the natives—which looked like a forty-foot owl.

I also passed a segment of road called Dead Man's Curve. I wondered how many dead man's curves there were in America. Probably thousands; the name applied every time a drunk or sleep-deprived driver drove over the side of a cliff.

There was a lot of challenging uphill walking, which even in my condition put me out of breath. On one segment I was passed by a very old man on a bicycle who was handling the climb better than I was.

I passed through the town of Laguna, where I stopped

at a rickety drive-in for a Laguna burger. Then I walked through Old Laguna, which was pretty much the same thing. I couldn't tell why they felt the need to distinguish Laguna from Old Laguna.

I ended my day in the town of Budville, where I stopped for dinner at King's Café Bar, then made my way to the Villa de Cubero Tourist Courts. A gas station and convenience store were in the front and red stucco hotel rooms were in back.

To my surprise, this remote desert oasis had had several brushes with celebrity. The woman in the store, who was also the owner, filled me in on the obscure resort's remarkable history. According to her, movie star Lucille Ball stayed there after leaving Desi Arnaz. The woman also claimed that Ernest Hemingway wrote part of *The Old Man and the Sea* while staying in one of their ten-by-twelve rooms. Maybe it's because this place was so remote and unlikely that it attracted famous people. Or, then again, maybe she just made it all up.

I spent the night in one of the old Villa Cubero rooms. The woman didn't know for sure which room Hemingway had stayed in, but, for whatever psychic deficit that drives us toward celebrity, I hoped it was the one I stayed in.

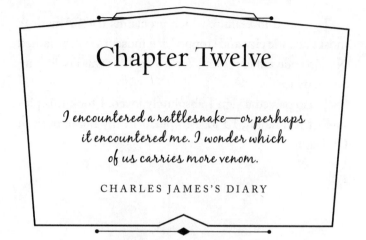

Chapter Twelve

I encountered a rattlesnake—or perhaps it encountered me. I wonder which of us carries more venom.

CHARLES JAMES'S DIARY

Other than cacti and the other three-thousand-plus species of desert plants, there's not much to see in western New Mexico. Over the next six days I walked through the towns of Grants, Prewitt, Thoreau, Fort Wingate, Gallup, and Manuelito, finally crossing over the border into Arizona near the border town (and Yellowhorse Giftshop) of Lupton.

I did have one exciting moment. Camping in the desert before Thoreau, I started to set up my camp in a place a rattlesnake had already claimed. It coiled and rattled—which I discovered sounded less like a rattle than a live electric wire—and I conceded him (or her) the campsite. I considered pelting the thing with rocks, then stopped myself. The reptile had more of a claim to the desert than I did.

I stopped in Gallup, which proclaims itself America's most patriotic city, and stopped at a museum for the famed Navajo code talkers from World War II. It was fascinating on many levels.

I also passed a sign I absolutely loved. I took this picture of it. Frankly, I'd love to put it in my home back in Chicago.

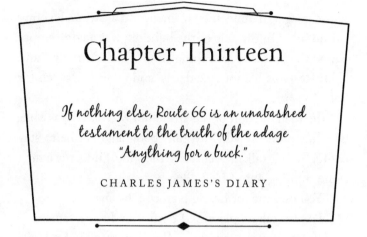

Chapter Thirteen

If nothing else, Route 66 is an unabashed testament to the truth of the adage "Anything for a buck."

CHARLES JAMES'S DIARY

I passed into Arizona without fanfare. There was no sign on 66 announcing it, so I just had to accept that I'd crossed my second-to-last border. Just past Allentown I got back on I-40 and made a brief stop at Fort Courage, advertised as "Home of *F Troop*," a popular 1960s TV show.

Before I started my journey my thought was "How hard could this be?" I expected an abundance of places to sleep and eat. What I didn't take into account was that 66 is a dead road, and I would spend more days in barren wasteland than in thriving towns. I had never eaten at so many gas stations.

My third day in Arizona I passed Stewart's Rock Shop, a junky little enclave created to catch travelers' eyes. Among other peculiarities was a large green dinosaur eating a (mannequin) woman, and a caveman riding a dinosaur. On the side of the building was a large empty pen with signs that said things like "Feed Ostriches" and "Not Responsible for Accidents" and finally "Ostrich for Sale."

The road in front of the attraction was barely passable, which is probably why my guidebook advised me to stay on 40. Still, I walked over to see the shop. Suddenly a man came running out of his trailer.

"You owe me for taking pictures!" he shouted.

"I'm not taking pictures. I don't even have a camera."

Undeterred, the guy said, "Then you owe me for looking."

I looked at him and said, "Is business that bad?" I gave him ten dollars, then went on my way.

I stopped for the day in the town of Holbrook, where there was a plethora of hotels and restaurants. I stayed at a Howard Johnson and ate dinner at the nearby Bear Café.

The next morning I walked through the rest of Holbrook. About a mile into my day I passed a large mural on the side of a building that read "Welcome Home, World." I also passed the cleverly named Empty Pockets Saloon. Around seven miles in there were signs advertising petrified wood for sale at Geronimo's, a tourist site with a teepee village.

I didn't know whether Geronimo had actually lived near the site, but I did know something about Geronimo, largely because he was a contemporary of my ancestor Jesse James. Both men had "Wanted Dead or Alive" posters. Geronimo wasn't even his name. His actual name was Goyahkla, which means "one who yawns."

Like my ancestor, Geronimo was a product of circumstance. He was originally a peaceful Apache medicine man, a shaman. In his thirties he went, with a group of Apache, to a small Mexican town to trade with the Mexican settlers. When he returned to his village he found that the Mexicans from a nearby town had attacked and killed everyone there, including his mother, wife, and three children.

The Apaches attacked the Mexican village in revenge. It was said that Geronimo fought so savagely that some of the Mexicans cried out to San Geronimo—Saint Jerome—for help. (There is some controversy surrounding this explanation, as Jerome was the patron saint of archeologists and librarians, not warriors.) Some just believe that his name was mispronounced. At any rate, the name stuck.

Geronimo spent the rest of his life seeking revenge—first against the Mexicans, then against the Americans entering the West. He was credited with supernatural powers, including the ability to heal the sick, slow time, and bring on rainstorms. He also had visions, many of which were proven true. At one point, nearly a quarter of the US Army took part in the final hunt for Geronimo, which made him the Osama bin Laden of his time.

He was the last Indian leader to formally surrender to the US military, and he spent the last twenty-three years of his life in Florida as a prisoner of war. Even though he was incarcerated, his fame continued to grow, and he made money selling autographs and bows and arrows to American tourists. He was eventually given permission to appear in the world's fairs and Wild West shows of the time, and even rode his horse in President Theodore Roosevelt's inauguration parade. He died in 1909 of pneumonia.

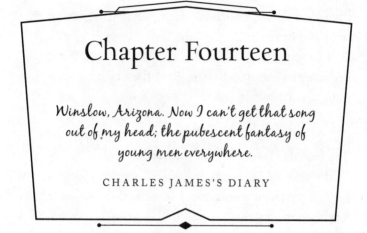

Chapter Fourteen

Winslow, Arizona. Now I can't get that song out of my head; the pubescent fantasy of young men everywhere.

CHARLES JAMES'S DIARY

The next town I passed through was Joseph City, established exactly fifty years before Route 66 was created. It is assumed the town was named after Mormon church founder Joseph Smith. A sign leading into the city read, "The Best Thing about Joseph City Is the People!"

From Joseph City I climbed over the interstate to get onto a frontage road and kept on it until I reached the town of Jackrabbit. The town's slogan is "If you haven't stopped at the Jackrabbit, you haven't been in the Southwest."

There is a very large sign pointing to Jackrabbit that says HERE IT IS. I'd seen pictures of the sign in my guidebook and at all the Route 66 museums I'd stopped at. From the hype I expected the jackrabbit statue to be roughly the size of Rhode Island, but it wasn't all that large or impressive.

I stopped at the Jackrabbit Trading Post for a cold drink and a candy bar, then spent the night camping just outside the town in the remains of a shed.

The next day I was back on I-40, walking along active railroad tracks, which tends to keep you awake. I lost track of how many trains passed me. I reached the town of Winslow, Arizona, by early afternoon.

Winslow was once one of the largest towns in northern Arizona, primarily because it was a railway hub—but once train travel slowed after World War II, it began advertising itself as a big Route 66 stop. Still, the town might have been forgotten if it weren't for a mention in a line from the Eagles song "Take It Easy."

Well I'm a standin' on a corner
in Winslow, Arizona
Such a fine sight to see

Had it been another band—say, Hootie & the Blowfish—it probably wouldn't have had much of a cultural impact. But the Eagles' *Greatest Hits* has gone on to be the bestselling album in history, recently dethroning *Thriller*, by the King of Pop, Michael Jackson.

The small town has answered the call of celebrity by building an impressive tourist attraction at the intersection of Second and Kinsley Streets. The cobblestone patch features a life-size bronze statue of the song's writer, Jackson Browne, holding a guitar in front of a road sign that reads:

STANDIN'

ON THE

CORNER

To the north of the statue is another bronze effigy, this one of Eagles front man Glenn Frey, which, I was told, was added shortly after Frey's death. There is a mural of a woman in a Ford truck in the window behind the statue and a fake bald eagle perched on the ledge of the windowsill above it. In the adjacent intersection is a massive Route 66 shield, and shops around the intersection sell Eagles paraphernalia and Winslow, Arizona, T-shirts.

"Take It Easy" loops continually on the outdoor speakers. I couldn't imagine what it would be like to be a town resident and hear the same song playing over and over for most of your life. I did the math. "Take It Easy" is roughly three minutes long. There are 1,440 minutes in a day (I used that in one of my stage presentations), which means it plays 480 times a day, or 3,360 times a week. That's 14,400 times a month, 175,200 times a year. Which means every five years eight and a half months, it plays a million times.

I stopped in the souvenir store across from the statue to get a bottle of water. I ended up buying a T-shirt and a guitar pick. When the woman in the store told me she'd heard the song a million times, I knew she wasn't exaggerating.

Every year more than a hundred thousand people stop to have their picture taken on that famous corner. One woman I watched took at least thirty different selfies. (How many pictures of yourself do you need?)

I spent the night at the luxurious and historic La Posada hotel, one of the few survivors from Winslow's more affluent railway days. Famous guests of the hotel include James Cagney, Franklin D. Roosevelt, Jimmy Stewart, Roy Rogers, Carole Lombard, Amelia Earhart, John Wayne, Betty Grable, Shirley Temple, Bob Hope, Will Rogers, Harry Truman, Gary Cooper, and at least two dozen more celebrities.

I ate dinner in the hotel's Turquoise Room, a beautiful dining room with turquoise rafters and stained-glass windows. Their advertisement boasts that you can sit and watch trains while you eat.

I stayed in a deluxe room with a whirlpool tub for only $169. The room was nice and unconventional, with a carved pine headboard, orange-and-white walls decorated with Zapotec rugs, and dark hardwood floors. It was a nice respite from camping in the desert.

Chapter Fifteen

I met a happily married couple, something I once might have considered as much an oddity as anything else I've encountered on Route 66.

CHARLES JAMES'S DIARY

I ate breakfast at the hotel, stopped at the market across the street for supplies, then took the one-way road out of Winslow. I followed the frontage road north of I-40 and put in a full twenty-mile day, the first in a while.

I ended up crossing the freeway to another famous Route 66 stop: Meteor City. There was an RV park just off the main road. I walked into the convenience store office to see if they allowed camping.

"Of course," the woman said kindly. "That's what we do. Are you walking?"

"Yes."

"Where from?"

"I started in Chicago."

"Lord Almighty," she said. "How many days did that take?"

"A few," I said. I hadn't added them up.

"Are you going to see the crater?"

"That depends on how far it is from here."

"Not far," she said. "About six miles."

"That's a twelve-mile walk," I said.

"Yes," she said. "It's very far. Maybe you could hitch a ride with someone. Most everyone here is headed that way."

I paid her twenty-five dollars for the night, and she took out a paper brochure of their campground and marked an X on a space across from the bathrooms.

"Your campsite is right there, across from the showers. I put you there because it's got grass and a shade tree and it's not too close to the others."

I thanked her, then walked around to the back of the building through a small gate. As I was setting up my tent a man walked up to me. He was about my age, red-haired and barrel chested with a pleasant face. He wore a black T-shirt with white printing that read,

SURELY NOT
EVERYBODY
WAS KUNG FU
FIGHTING

"How's it going?" he asked.

I stopped what I was doing and stood. "Well, thank you."

"It's pretty warm out."

"It is the desert."

"Indeed. Where are you coming from?"

"Chicago."

"Hiking Sixty-Six?"

"How'd you guess?"

"It's a bucket-list thing. We're on it, too. Not hiking; we've got the RV. Walking in this heat would probably kill me." He laughed. "Actually, just the walking would kill me." He extended his hand. "My name is Norm. Norm Stiles from Dayton."

I shook his hand. "I'm Charles."

"Pleased to know you, Charles. My wife and I are over yonder in the tan Winnebago."

I looked over at a midsize RV with a canopy extending from one side. There was a smoking barbecue grill near the passenger door.

"As you can see, I've got my Traeger fired up. I've been smoking a pork butt for six hours, and it's just the missus and I. I came to invite you to have dinner with us."

I'm embarrassed to say that I questioned his motives. But a hot meal is a hot meal, and it was that or the cold burrito I'd bought in the convenience store.

"Thank you. That sounds great."

"Excellent. I'm about twenty minutes out, so come on over whenever you're ready. I've got some cold Buds in the ice chest. See you in a few." He started to turn, then said, "It was Charles, right?"

"Yes."

"Hope you join us." He turned and walked back to his RV.

I finished setting up my tent, then, taking my pack with me, walked over to their campsite. Their RV was about twenty feet long and parked on a base of gravel next to water and sewer hookups.

In front of the vehicle, under a canvas shade, sat a woman. She was about Norm's age, wide-faced, blond with green eyes. She smiled and stood as I approached. "Hi. You're Charles?"

"Yes, ma'am."

"I'm Judy."

"It's nice to meet you, Judy."

"Likewise. Grab a chair. Norm will be right out."

"Thank you." I sat on one of the chairs. "Nice setup you have here."

"All the comforts of home," she said.

Norm walked out of the RV carrying a plate. "Ah, you made it." He set the plate he was carrying on a small portable table next to his grill. "Judy made her famous blue-ribbon baked beans. I'll put your pack inside, if you like."

"Thank you." I shrugged off my pack and Norm set it inside the door.

"Help yourself to a beer," he said. "Bud Light okay? Judy's been after me to take a few pounds off."

She shook her head and looked at me. "I've never said that." She grinned. "I might have thought it. But I never said it."

I grabbed a can of beer from the ice chest and then sat back while Norm pulled the pork from the grill. He cut a small piece from the end and offered it on the tines of a fork to Judy. She pulled it off with her fingers and popped it into her mouth. "Tender," she said.

"As our love," Norm said. He cut the pork into slices, the juices dripping over the side of the wooden carving board.

Judy smiled, then turned to me. "Come and get it."

"Thanks," I said. I grabbed a plate and filled it with food, then returned to my chair. Norm turned off the grill and, filling his plate, sat down with us.

"This is the good life," he said.

Judy nodded in agreement.

"Thank you for the invitation," I said. "Everything is delicious."

"Our pleasure," Judy said.

I enjoyed watching the two of them interact. There was something intriguing about their relationship. Maybe it was something as simple as the fact that they liked each other.

As the evening drew on, I asked Norm, "How long have you been married?"

"Forever," he said.

Judy reached over and slapped his leg. "Thirty-five years."

"Thirty-five years," I echoed. "You seem like you have a good marriage."

"I kind of like the guy," Judy said. Then she added, "Wasn't always that way."

He sighed. "That's for sure."

"Really?" I asked.

"For years the wife and I struggled."

"That's an understatement," she said, smiling slightly.

Norm groaned. "Seemed the longer we were married the more difficult things got. The tension between us got so bad that whenever I'd go away on business it was a relief, for both of us. At least while I was gone. 'Course, we always paid for it on reentry.

"Our fighting became so constant that it was difficult to even imagine a peaceful relationship. We were on the edge of divorce, and more than once we discussed it."

"'Discussed' is a nice way of saying it," Judy said, squeezing her husband's hand.

"So what happened?" I asked.

"I was on the road, in Toledo, when things came to a head. We had just had another big fight on the phone and Judy had hung up on me. I was alone and frustrated and angry.

"That's when I turned to God. Or turned *on* God. Maybe shouting at God isn't prayer, maybe it is—but whatever I was engaged in I'll never forget it. I was standing in the shower of a Motel 6, yelling at God that I couldn't do it anymore. As much as I hated the idea of divorce, the pain of being together was just too much.

"I was also confused. I couldn't figure out why marriage was so hard. Deep down I knew that Judy was a good person. And I was a good person. So why couldn't we get along? Why wouldn't she change?

"Finally, I just sat down in the shower and began to cry. That's when a voice said to me, *You can't change her. You can only change yourself.* At that moment I thought, *If I can't change* her, *God, then change* me. I prayed late into the night. I prayed the next day on the drive home. I prayed as I walked in the door to a cold wife who barely even acknowledged me.

"That night, as we lay in our bed, inches from each other yet miles apart, I knew what I had to do.

"The next morning I rolled over in bed next to Judy and said, 'How can I make your day better?'

"Judy looked at me like I'd lost my mind and said, 'What?'

"What can I do to make your day better?'

"'You can't,' she said. 'Why are you asking that?'

"'Because I mean it,' I said. 'I just want to know what I can do to make your day better.'

"Then she said, 'You want to do something? Go clean the kitchen.' I think she expected me to get mad."

Judy nodded. "I was socking it to him."

"Instead I just bit my lip and said, 'Okay.' I got up and cleaned the kitchen.

"The next day I asked the same thing. 'What can I do to make your day better?'"

"I said, 'Clean the garage,'" Judy said. "I was being mean."

Norm nodded. "I knew she was trying to start something. And normally I would have blown a gasket. Instead I said, 'Okay.' I got up and for the next two hours cleaned the garage. Judy wasn't sure what to think.

"The next morning I said, 'What can I do to make your day better?' She said, 'Nothing! You can't do anything. Stop saying that.'

"I said, 'I'm sorry, but I can't. I made a commitment to myself. What can I do to make your day better?'

"She said, 'Why are you doing this?'

"I said, 'Because I care about you and our marriage.'

"The next morning, I asked again. And the next. And the next. Then, during the second week, a miracle occurred. As I asked the question Judy's eyes welled up with tears. Then she broke down crying. When she could speak she said, 'Please stop asking me that. You're not the problem. I'm hard to live with. I don't know why you stay with me.'

"I lifted her chin until she was looking in my eyes and I said, 'It's because I love you. What can I do to make your day better?'

She said, 'I should be asking you that.'

"'You should,' I said. 'But right now, I need to be the change. You need to know how much you mean to me.'"

I looked over at Judy. She was beaming. "It was amazing," she said.

"She put her head against my chest and said, 'I'm sorry I've been so mean.'

"'I love you,' I said. 'I love you,' she said back.

"The next morning when I asked, 'What can I do to make your day better?' she said, 'Can we just spend some time together?'"

"He kept asking for more than a month," Judy said.

Norm nodded. "We began having meaningful discussions on what we wanted from life and how we could make each other happier," he said. "I can't say that we never fought again, but our fights changed. They lacked the energy they'd once had. We just didn't have it in us to hurt each other anymore."

He looked at Judy. "We've been married for more than thirty years. I not only love her, I like her. I like being with her. I need her. We've finally learned how to take care of each other." He nodded slowly. "Marriage is *hard*. But so is everything else that's important in my life. To have a partner in life is a gift. I've also learned that marriage, if we let it, can help heal us of our most unlovable parts. And we all have unlovable parts."

I sat there thinking about what he'd said, and about all my unlovable parts.

"Thank you for sharing that," I said.

"Our pleasure," Norm replied.

"And dinner. That was . . . epic."

"Glad you enjoyed it," Judy said. "It was nice to have your company."

Norm said, "I don't know if you've seen the crater yet, but we're going in the morning. Would you like a lift?"

I thought a moment, then said, "Yes. I'd like that. What time?"

"The place opens at eight, so we'll leave a few minutes before that. We're not ones to tarry."

"I'll be here at a quarter to."

"You might as well come at seven and get some breakfast," Judy said. "I'm making Belgian waffles."

"I'm not one to turn down Belgian waffles," I said. "I'll see you then. Thanks again. Good night."

"Good night, partner," Norm said.

I walked back to my tent, their story still playing in my mind. *What can I do to make your day better?* I wish I had heard that story a decade ago. But then, would I have even listened?

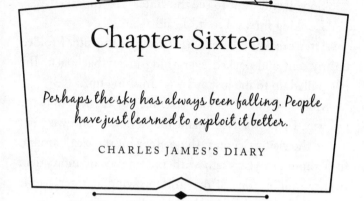

Chapter Sixteen

Perhaps the sky has always been falling. People have just learned to exploit it better.

CHARLES JAMES'S DIARY

I woke early the next morning and took a shower in the camp facilities. It was a few minutes after seven when I walked to Norm and Judy's camp. Norm was standing next to the grill cooking bacon.

"Good morning," I said.

"Morning. How'd you sleep?"

"Well. Something smells good."

"Bacon always smells good. It's brought down more vegetarians than all the other meats combined."

Judy walked out of the RV. "Morning, Charles."

"Good morning."

"Can I get you some coffee?"

"Yes, please."

"Cream and sugar?"

"Just cream."

"So you still want to see the crater?" Norm asked.

"Looking forward to it," I said.

After breakfast I went back to my campsite. I folded up my tent and packed everything in my backpack. The RV pulled up to me just as I was finishing up.

Meteor Crater is about six miles of desert from the freeway. I paid for Norm and Judy's tickets and we went inside the visitors' center. The meteor hit the earth around fifty thousand years ago with the energy of more than twenty million tons of dynamite, leaving a crater a mile across and more than five hundred feet deep.

The exhibit was worth seeing. There were pieces of the meteor on display, twisted chunks of metal that looked like artwork. NASA had once used the crater for training, and their exhibit included an Apollo test capsule and pictures of the astronauts.

I had always assumed that a meteor was an anomaly, a rare visitor from another realm. What I didn't know was that at any given time there are millions of asteroids circling the Earth like bees around a hive. In other words, the end could come at any time.

We were there for almost two hours. Finally we drove back out, stopping the RV in front of the RV park.

"Sure we can't take you anywhere?" Judy asked.

"No," I said. "The walk's the thing."

"More profound words were never spoken," Norm said. He handed me a business card. "Call me when you make it."

"I will. Thank you."

"God speed," Judy said.

"*Con Dios*," I replied.

I stepped back and the big RV lumbered back onto the road, then down the freeway on-ramp. I was glad to have met them.

Chapter Seventeen

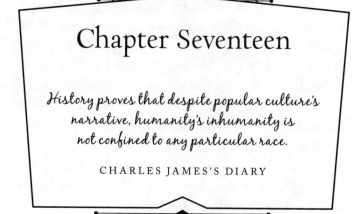

History proves that despite popular culture's narrative, humanity's inhumanity is not confined to any particular race.

CHARLES JAMES'S DIARY

An hour into the day I passed the ghost town of Two Guns. If there are places in the world with the power to attract evil, Two Guns is one of them. The town's first recorded infamy was in 1878, when a group of Apache Indians hid in a cave from their Navajo enemies. Unfortunately they were discovered and the Navajos lit sagebrush fires at the cave's entrance to either kill or smoke the Apaches out, shooting any who tried to escape. Forty-two Apaches were killed.

Just a year later, Billy the Kid and his gang established a hiding place near the town. Two Guns was a popular site, since it was one of the easiest ways to cross the appropriately named Canyon Diablo, the Devil's Canyon.

When the Santa Fe Railway began laying tracks across the area, the Two Guns settlement became a wild place of drifters and outlaws. Not surprisingly, the train was robbed of nearly two hundred thousand dollars in silver, gold, and currency. The thieves were caught, but less than one hundred dollars was ever recovered. One of the thieves disclosed before his death that the loot had been buried in the canyon rim near Two Guns.

In 1922 the town experienced a small rebirth when Earle and Louise Cundiff purchased 320 acres and built a store, a restaurant, and gas pumps.

Soon after, a white man calling himself Chief Crazy Thunder leased property from the Cundiffs and built his own zoo with desert animals he collected himself—mountain lions, coral snakes, Gila monsters, and other killers. He then expanded his zoo with a tour of the death cave and sold Apache skulls as souvenirs.

Nineteen twenty-six heralded the arrival of Route 66 through the town, which brought potential wealth. Cundiff and the chief got into an argument about his lease, and the renter shot his unarmed landlord to death. Today all that's left of the town is a burned-out service station, painted grain mills, and an abandoned, graffiti-covered KAMP lodge.

Later that afternoon I reached the Twin Arrows Casino Resort. The casino was a mile from the freeway and a welcome oasis from the desert heat. Like most Native American–owned casinos, it had a nature theme. This one was Earth, Wind, Fire, and Water—the four elements displayed in various artistic designs in the spacious lobby's décor.

The rooms were inexpensive and nice. They had a nice all-you-can-eat buffet. After eating my fill, I retired to the sports bar to watch the Chicago Cubs get spanked.

Chapter Eighteen

I wrote my own Burma Shave poem: He who lives / like he won't die / won't find a mansion / in the sky.

CHARLES JAMES'S DIARY

The next day was simple walking, though traffic increased as I neared the populous town of Flagstaff. At fourteen miles I entered the Flagstaff city limits, and reached the town itself by late afternoon.

Flagstaff is a populated mountain town built along the southwestern edge of the Colorado Plateau just south of the San Francisco Peaks—the highest mountain range in Arizona. For many years it was the largest town between Albuquerque and the West Coast.

Flagstaff began as a lumber town, which is no surprise, since it borders the largest ponderosa pine forest in the United States. It was named after a pine flagpole made by a scouting party celebrating the US centennial in 1876.

As I left the freeway, I could see the Flagstaff Mall to

the north of me. I went inside, which was a little strange, since I hadn't been around that many people for a while. I found the mall's canned music disturbing to my psyche as well.

I stopped at the Foot Locker and purchased a new pair of walking shoes and socks, which I put on immediately, disposing of the overly worn ones I had been wearing by tossing them in the store's trash can.

A young woman at the store recommended a restaurant called Fat Olives, which is where I ate dinner. I had their Adovada pizza, a spicy pork tenderloin pizza with roasted onions. I spent the night at a Holiday Inn Express not far from the restaurant.

I started walking early the next morning. Large portions of Route 66 still exist in Flagstaff, and I regained the route just a few miles from the hotel. Leaving the city I found the walking conditions optimal, as the road remained wide and the air cool, due to the elevation and the ubiquitous forest. There was some road construction, which in this rare case played to my advantage as it opened an entire lane for walking.

It was along this stretch that I encountered my first road sign for Los Angeles. It hit me hard, reminding me that there was an end to my journey. What would happen when I saw Monica? I still had no idea what I'd say.

A few hours later I was back on I-40 and then crossed the Arizona divide. Oddly, someone had left a nice couch on the side of the road. It was just sitting there as pristine as if it were on the display floor of the local furniture emporium. I sat on it just because. I wondered what its story was.

I camped that night in the woods. There was nice tree coverage, and in spite of the previous two nights' hotel stays, the camping was nice. I could have used that couch, though.

⁂

The next week was beautiful walking but uneventful. The first day was Williams, with its Bearizona Wildlife Park. Williams was a well-preserved historic district with a Masonic lodge, historic train depot, and Grand Canyon railway. There were a surprising number of hotels. Williams was another one of those towns that was bypassed when I-40 was built but refused to dry up.

The only thing of interest over the next few days was the return of Burma Shave signs:

T'WOULD BE MORE FUN

TO GO BY AIR

IF WE COULD PUT

THESE SIGNS UP THERE

HE TRIED TO CROSS

AS FAST TRAIN NEARED

DEATH DIDN'T DRAFT HIM

HE VOLUNTEERED

Outside the town of Seligman was a long string of telephone poles that resembled old telegraph poles. They were unusually close to each other, all with a single crossbar. From a distance it made the valley look like a giant cemetery.

The temperature was consistently getting warmer as I approached Needles, California, the hottest and likely the most difficult part of my walk.

THE ONE WHO DRIVES

WHEN HE'S BEEN DRINKING

DEPENDS ON YOU

TO DO THE THINKING

IF HUGGING ON HIGHWAYS

IS YOUR SPORT

TRADE IN YOUR CAR

FOR A DAVENPORT

I spent the night in Seligman at the historic Route 66 Motel and ate dinner at the Roadkill 66 Café right next to the motel. The restaurant featured such delicacies as Poodles and Noodles, Roadside Remnants, Road Toad, Caddie-grilled Patty, and Swirl of Squirrel, their menu congruent with their slogan: "You kill it—We grill it."

Unfortunately, I ordered their barbecue beef sandwich, which, frankly, looked like roadkill. I wouldn't recommend it.

The next day I encountered more Burma Shave signs.

LISTEN BIRDS

THESE SIGNS COST MONEY

SO ROOST AWHILE

BUT DON'T GET FUNNY

And another:

IF DAISIES ARE YOUR

FAVORITE FLOWER

KEEP PUSHIN' UP

THOSE MILES PER HOUR

And another:

CATTLE CROSSING

MEANS GO SLOW

THAT OLD BULL

IS SOME COW'S BEAU

(Amusingly, there were a group of cows gathered together near this particular row of signs.)

SURE, YOU CAN GO

A MILE A MINUTE

BUT THERE IS NO

FUTURE IN IT

That night I reached the town of Hackberry. As I entered the town, I passed a house with a hand-painted sign out front:

BURT'S COUNTRY DANCING

I thought the idea of a guy named Burt converting his home into a dance hall in the middle of nowhere was so funny that I was half-tempted to ring the doorbell and check it out. Fortunately, I was *more* than half-tempted not to, afraid that someone might try to make me dance. Not even Monica could do that.

The next morning I passed the Hackberry General Store, which had the largest collection of Route 66 paraphernalia I'd seen anywhere on my journey—which was likely why it also had the largest infestation of tourists, mostly European.

A middle-aged woman with long gray hair sat outside the door under a canopy playing a guitar. She had a small amplifier and a table with CDs on it. I bought one, then gave it away to a French couple as I left the grounds.

I stopped for supplies and water at the Ranchero Market. In spite of the rising heat, I was making good time, and I continued pushing ahead to Kingman.

Around four, I passed the Kingman Airport and Industrial Park. An electric sign in front of the bank read 97 degrees. I was exhausted and soaked in sweat. I had walked a marathon today.

I stopped at the first hotel I found, a Days Inn. I was hungry but too tired to walk anywhere. I asked the woman at the hotel counter about nearby restaurants. When she found out that I'd walked twenty-six miles that day, she arranged for the hotel shuttle to drive me to the Kingman Chophouse. I came back to the hotel and soaked in the tub.

Chapter Nineteen

I had an experience today that I'm not sure how to process. It's well said that there are more things in heaven and earth than are dreamt of in our philosophies.

CHARLES JAMES'S DIARY

I woke the next morning with sore legs. I ate a large pancake breakfast next door at JB's, then headed west. I was now sixty-three miles from Needles, California, and I could feel anxiety rising in my chest for two reasons. One, I would be crossing the Mojave Desert on foot, something no one in their right mind would look forward to, let alone attempt. But I had a greater anxiety. I was approaching the last border. I was just three days from California. I was going to finish this journey. Then what?

Kingman's an interesting place. I hadn't seen a town that large embrace its Route 66 history since Joliet, way back in Illinois. Three miles through the town I came to a water tower painted with a massive Route 66 shield above the words:

WELCOME TO KINGMAN

HEART OF HISTORIC ROUTE 66

I passed another vintage car dealership. Something about the route made me want to connect to the automobiles of the road's era. I went inside to admire the cars. Without any provocation, the man working there launched into a political tirade, concluding with *This country is going to hell in a handbasket.*

He asked me what I was driving. When I told him I wasn't, he didn't believe me. Then he asked me where I was going. When I told him he just shook his head.

"You taking I-40 or the Oatman Highway?"

"Oatman," I said.

He shook his head again. "Take a lot of water, my friend. Gallons. Three or four."

A gallon of water weighs just a little over eight pounds. That meant increasing my load by more than thirty pounds. In spite of his political ranting, I took his advice about the water.

I left Kingman on westbound I-40. A few miles later I crossed over the Holy Moses Wash, then exited the freeway for the Oatman Highway, which brought me back to Historic Route 66.

This was a byway that clearly wasn't much traveled, and there weren't any amenities for dozens of miles. The only town my map claimed was the eclectic Oatman. Peculiarly, the road sparkled like glass. I actually crouched down to examine the paved road, which was intermingled with specks of a black, onyx-like stone.

I passed a sign that read: "No Motorcycles and No Trucks over 40 Feet Allowed on This Road." I could understand why large trucks weren't allowed, but not the motorcycles. Maybe they didn't want motorcycle gangs.

There was nothing to see but cacti. I could only imagine what the settlers felt seeing the mountains ahead, knowing that California was on the other side.

It was during this stretch that I had an experience I still don't know how to make sense of. I don't care whether you believe me or not, because, frankly, I'm still not sure if I believe it. Chalk it up to the heat if you'd like.

I was walking alongside the raised railroad track, headed toward the Black Mountains town of Oatman. There was nothing to see but the occasional washout and signs to watch for flooding, which, considering the arid vastness of the land around me, seemed about as appropriate as a Smokey the Bear forest fire warning in Antarctica.

Then, in the distance, I saw someone walking toward me—a slight, blurry wave in the intense heat. As he got closer, I could see that it was a man in a white robe and sandals. It occurred to me that he didn't have a pack, or water. When he was fifty or so feet in front of me he locked eyes with me. "Good afternoon," he said.

"A hot one," I replied. "Do you need water?"

"That's kind of you to offer. You've made progress on your journey." Then he stopped, looked me in the eyes, and said, "Remember, Charles, the road *is* the destination." Then he just walked on.

The road is the destination. How did he know my name? But when I turned around to ask him, he was gone. I just stood there looking around me. There was no possible place he could have hidden. The encounter shook me. Was I delirious with sunstroke?

I was glad I had listened to the ranting man in Kingman, since otherwise I would have run out of water by then. There was truly nothing out there. I camped for the night in a floodplain on the opposite side of the railroad tracks. As I lay in my tent, I couldn't get the old man off my mind. *The road is the destination.* Had I really seen someone?

Chapter Twenty

This afternoon, I, along with a pack of burros, walked into Oatman, thereby increasing the town's jackass population by one.

CHARLES JAMES'S DIARY

Around noon of the next day I came upon a welcome oasis, a refurbished 66 gas station and museum enticingly named Cool Springs. The building was a well-kept gift shop with a wood-and-mortared-stone façade. A large, bright-red sign on its roof advertised "CABINS" and "TASTY FOODS."

In addition to the American and Arizona flags on the front flagpole, the flags of a dozen other countries lined the building. I took my time inside, enjoying the air conditioning and filling up on both food and water, with several sleeves of crackers and a couple of candy bars for the road ahead.

Leaving Cool Springs, 66 rose into Sitgreaves Pass—a narrow mountain pass largely without guardrails. It was difficult, even treacherous walking, a barely two-lane road with little or no shoulder. It was also one of the most beautiful roads I'd traveled, a scenic byway of blackened stone and miles of cacti.

A few miles up the road I passed a sign that read:

WATCH FOR DONKEYS

The road took me past what I guessed was a modern gold mine—at least the road to it was Gold Mine Road—though, as far as I could see, there was no one working the site.

About an hour later I came to a settlement of motor homes leading into the mountaintop town of Oatman.

Historic Oatman began as a mining camp claimed by a mountain man and prospector named Johnny Moss. The prospector's fortunes changed when he struck a major vein of ore, eventually producing more than $10 million of gold.

Possibly with the exception of the town's residents, Oatman looked like it hadn't changed much over the preceding century. When I entered the main thoroughfare I understood the "Watch for Donkeys" sign, as there were burros everywhere. Several of them approached me, aggressively nosing me for a handout, which I obliged, giving them some of the Ritz crackers I had purchased in Cool Springs.

The donkeys were clearly the town's mascots, and the names of the local businesses all reflected their presence:

The Bucktooth Burro
The Classy Ass
Jackass Junction

I spent the night at the Oatman Hotel, Restaurant & Saloon. The saloon was decorated, interestingly, with currency. Thousands of dollar bills—donated over the years by the saloon's guests—were hung on the walls.

The food was good and the room comfortable, though admittedly the best part of both was the air conditioning.

The next three days' walking was hot and uneventful. Actually, the hot *was* eventful. It was like walking through a blast furnace. The landscape reflected the climate, appearing more lunar than earthly. Every few hours I would stop and pour water over my head; it would evaporate in minutes. Fortunately there were enough watering holes to keep myself hydrated. I don't know how the pioneers made it through this area.

The most peculiar things I noticed in the desert were hundreds of rock stacks, usually in columns of three or four. I couldn't make sense of it. They might have been grave markers. Did people come out here to bury their animals?

Chapter Twenty-One

I crossed my last state border into Needles, California. If flesh could melt, I'd be a puddle somewhere along the side of the road. I met a man claiming to be an author, but he may have just been a mirage.

CHARLES JAMES'S DIARY

By the third day from Oatman, Route 66 rejoined with I-40 where it crossed the Colorado River and then the state border into California. I had made it to my last state. I was too hot to make a big deal out of it.

In spite of the heat, the road was nice and smooth with wide shoulders, the Colorado River flowing peacefully to my right. Halfway through my day I stopped at an inspection station, where I had a peculiar conversation with the inspector.

Inspector: You're walking?
Me: (*Did you have to ask?*) Yes.

Inspector: Do you have any fruit?

Me: I have two apples.

Inspector: Good. You're going to need them.

It felt like someone kept turning up the thermostat. My sunburned skin was as dark as it was going to get. I took out one of my T-shirts and wrapped it around my head like a Bedouin head scarf.

At least six times, people, amazed that I was walking through this inferno, stopped their cars to offer me a ride or, at least, water. I never refused the water, even if it was just to dump over my head.

Fourteen miles into my day I staggered into Needles City. An electric marquee outside a bank put the temperature at 118 degrees.

There was a covered wagon near the entrance of the city with the town name painted on it. Below it was a sign that read

NEEDLES

20 MILES FROM WATER

2 FEET FROM HELL

I walked through town, stopping to eat at a Route 66 classic: the Wagon Wheel Restaurant. As I sat there in the diner, reading up on the city in my guidebook, I noticed a man looking at me. I guessed he was in his late forties. He spoke to me, and we started a conversation. He said he was a novelist and was working on a book about Route 66. He was fascinated that I'd just walked most of it.

As we talked, he recognized me. He knew of my career and book and my supposed death, though he promised to keep my secret. He said he might be interested in writing my story. His name was Richard Paul Evans. His career started when he wrote a Christmas story that struck a national chord and sold millions of copies.

I gave him my email but told him that I couldn't promise anything because I still didn't know how my story ended. He said he understood. I guess we'll see where that goes. (If you're reading this, you already know.)

I spent the night sleeping above the covers at the Needles Budget Inn.

I started the next morning a couple of hours before sunrise. The temperature was already 90 degrees, and it wasn't even 6:00 a.m. I soon found that everyone else had the same idea, at least those who worked in the elements, and landscapers and construction workers were already well into their day. I ate breakfast at the Giggling Cactus, then set back out along I-40.

As I walked, I kept thinking about the author I met in Needles. I wondered how my story was going to end and if, in the final act, it would be worth telling. I supposed that was up to me.

I kept on walking through the blistering heat. Usually the most interesting stories are born of suffering, but not in this case. The next week was brutally painful but with little to write about. At times I felt like I was traveling through an apocalyptic wasteland. Or hell. I passed dry lakebeds crusted with minerals, lava rock, and the occasional home surrounded by its own landfill of broken-down cars and appliances.

I remember passing an abandoned building with a spray-painted message: "Smile, there's hope."

You would think that after walking through the Mojave Desert—hot-enough-to-melt-the-soles-of-your-shoes heat—I'd be used to it. But I wasn't. You never really get used to it. Hot is hot.

I kept myself going by telling myself that I wasn't far from Barstow, civilization, and air conditioning.

Chapter Twenty-Two

Today, in Barstow, I ran into someone who recognized me. Fortunately, he didn't know I was dead. I'd like to be there when he finds out.

CHARLES JAMES'S DIARY

I reached Barstow a little past noon on the tenth day from Oatman. All I wanted was an oasis with a swimming pool, which I found coming into town at a Ramada Inn. The hotel had light, cream-colored stucco walls and clay terra-cotta tiles and was surrounded by tall palm trees that rose higher than the building. It had an outdoor swimming pool, and from what I could see, there was no one in it, which appealed to me. Swimming pools at the family-branded hotels usually came with screaming hordes of children.

Barstow was not unfamiliar to me. I had presented there twice before, but back then I had stayed with my entourage at the Club at Big Bear Village, which was nice but way too far to walk for a few hours of luxury.

I went inside the Ramada and booked a room, took the elevator to the third floor, where I dropped my backpack, then went back out and walked about a mile west down Interstate 15 to the famous Barstow Station, a curiously constructed indoor shopping and travel stop complete with out-of-service Santa Fe railcars and the usual list of fast-food eateries.

It was cool inside, and the air conditioners provided a continual ambience of white noise. In addition to the fast-food outlets there was a liquor store, a Jed's Jerky, the Hollywood shop, Oriental shop, and Double R Gifts, which boasted the largest candy counter on the I-15 freeway.

I stopped at a Dunkin' Donuts for dinner, ordering two chicken salad croissants and my favorite donuts—a French cruller and an old-fashioned cake donut, along with a coffee. I got my food and walked to the dining area—a long, narrow section built to resemble a train car. I sat down at a small table for two to eat.

I ate the donuts first (there are no words in the English language that can truly describe the pleasure of a warm cruller) and had started on my first sandwich when I noticed at a booth just a few yards from me a little girl standing precariously in her high chair. There were no adults around, just two little boys, one of whom was lying across the bench on his back kicking the side of the little girl's high chair. Amazingly, she hadn't fallen. The floor was cement, and, from the height of the chair, she could be seriously hurt.

As the boy brought his foot back again to kick the

chair, I jumped up and grabbed the little girl by the arms. "Stop that," I said. "She could crack open her head."

The boy looked at me in terror.

"Did you hear me?" I said.

"Okay," he said, recoiling against the wall.

The people around me looked on uncomfortably. They looked anxious that I had intervened where I didn't belong. I sat the little girl back down in the chair.

As I walked back to my table, a man at the table behind me stood, his eyes locked on mine. There were five others at the table, three of them children. I wondered if he wanted trouble. I looked into his eyes, expecting him to turn away, but he didn't. Finally I pulled a Robert De Niro. "Are you looking at me?"

His eyes squinted. "Charles?"

Hearing my name struck me like a ball peen hammer. Outside of Amanda, no one had called me by my name in months. I had no idea who he was, even though he apparently knew who I was. For all I knew, he could have been one of a thousand attendees sitting in the back of the auditorium at my last Barstow seminar.

". . . Charles James?"

Didn't he know that I was supposed to be dead?

He stepped closer. "It is you," he said, his lips rising in a broad smile. "The one and only Mr. Charles James, the rainmaker himself. What a small world, running into you here in Barstow."

"How are you?" I asked, still having no idea who he was.

A grin crossed his face as his eyes scanned me. "You don't remember me, do you?" Before I could answer he said, "That's all right, Jimmy. There have been a lot of us crossing your stage. It's Dave Freed. We were on the circuit together back in aught seven."

With the help of his prompt I remembered him, even though he didn't look like he once had. For one, he was wearing shorts and a Harley-Davidson T-shirt instead of a crisply starched shirt, silk tie, and expensive suit. Also, it had been nearly a decade, and he hadn't aged especially well. He'd lost half of his hair and gained a few dozen pounds.

"Right," I said. "Dave. You were selling those *protect your assets* packages."

"That's right, that's right. Choose it or lose it," he said, smiling and slapping his butt. "I'm covering your Assetts."

"Memorable slogan."

"Unforgettable, right? So what brings you through Barstow? I didn't see any advertisement that you were coming." I deduced by now that he didn't know I was supposed to be dead.

"Just taking a little time off from the circuit," I said.

"Good on you. Not sure that Barstow would top my bucket list, but glad you've got some downtime. I've been taking a little time off myself. The wife and I have been staying with my daughter and son-in-law in London."

"London, England?"

"Not London, Ohio," he said. "My daughter married a Brit. He's got a great job there, corporate attorney for

Dow. I tell you, it's been just fantastic. Those Brits know how to live. More Michelin-rated restaurants per square mile than anywhere else in the world."

"So what brings you to Barstow?"

"I just got back to the States last week. Wife and I thought we'd make a quick hop to see the grandkids before heading home to Phoenix. Where are you headed?"

At least that explained why he didn't know I was supposed to be dead. But it wouldn't be long before he found out. All he had to do was tell someone that he'd run into me. I decided to play with his head a little. I gazed deeply into his eyes, then repeated, "Where am I headed? Now that's a good question, isn't it?"

"I thought so," he said.

"Where am I headed? Nowhere, my friend. Nowhere and *everywhere*. Just wandering. Don't you know that sinners are destined to wander the earth? Just like Marley."

His brow furrowed. "Marley? You mean that guy from Steubenville who was selling those five-in-one business branding packages?"

"Jacob Marley," I said. "As in *The Christmas Carol.*"

"Oh, right," he said, his brow falling with confusion. "Scrooge's partner."

I nodded. "Jacob Marley. And what he said was true. Mankind was my *business*. The common welfare was my *business*. Mercy, forbearance, charity, they were all my business. Not selling pipe dreams of wealth to people who couldn't afford their light bills."

Freed looked at me anxiously, no doubt wondering if he should laugh or run. He chose the latter. "Well, we were just headed out. Good luck with your . . . wandering. I'm sure we'll run into each other before too long. It's a small world."

"Smaller than you could possibly imagine," I said. "Oh, you'll see me again, my friend. On this side or the next, we will most definitely meet again."

By that point I was certain that he regretted approaching me and was sure that I'd lost my mind. "Okay, good, good with that. Look forward to . . . You take care. Good seeing you." He gathered up his clan and hurried off. Now he would definitely tell others about our meeting. He might even google me. I kind of wished I could be there when he learned about my death.

I chuckled to myself as I sat back down and finished my sandwiches. Afterward I bought a few sundries: toothpaste, sunscreen, and Advil at Double R Gifts, then stopped at the jerky shop and bought several packages of spicy brisket and habañero jerky.

I took my purchases back to the Ramada. I traded my clothing for my swimming suit, then went down to the pool. The hotel's pool area was large and well groomed, surrounded by cacti and orange-fruited kumquat trees in terra-cotta pots.

It wasn't vacant anymore. Two women sat in the hot tub, which, considering the heat, struck me as unpleasant.

I draped my towel over a reclining vinyl-strapped chair

and jumped into the deep end of the pool. I could imagine my skin sizzling as it hit the water.

The water felt heavenly. I swam around for at least half an hour before getting out and lying back in the recliner to dry off. An hour later I went back up to my room.

As I lay on top of the bed, I heard the muffled ring of a cell phone. The phone rang six times and then stopped. I thought the phone was outside my room and wondered why no one had answered it. It was only half a minute before it started ringing again. Suddenly it occurred to me that the sound was coming from my phone—the one Amanda had bought for me in Amarillo. It was the first time anyone had called me on it, so not only had I forgotten that I had it but I also didn't know what its ring tone sounded like. I dug through my pack until I found it.

"Amanda?"

"Hi. How are you?"

"Good."

"Where are you?"

"Barstow."

"Barstow. Are you staying at the Big Bear?"

I was always amazed that she remembered every place we had ever been. "No. It's too far off the path. I'm at a Ramada. Do you remember a guy named Freed?"

"Of course. Dave Freed, sold the Protect your Assets packages."

"I ran into him."

"Did he recognize you?"

"Yes."

"What did you say? I mean, how did you explain your . . . existence?"

"He's been out of the country, so he didn't know I'm supposed to be dead."

She was quiet a moment, then her voice fell. "Speaking of . . . I've got some bad news. McKay passed away."

The news hit me with force. The last time McKay and I had spoken was in St. Louis, when he told me he was dying and that he'd forgiven me. I had also, at a distance, seen him at my funeral, as he returned my betrayal with kindness. I had assumed that I would have time to apologize to him after my walk. I suppose it's always that way. We always assume that there's tomorrow to make things right. Maybe that's why the Bible says to not *procrastinate your day of repentance*.

"When did he pass?" I asked.

Amanda sniffed, though I'm not sure if it was from emotion. "This morning. Early, like six Eastern Time. Marissa called me."

I knew that Amanda's feelings must have been as complicated as mine, if not more so. She had been McKay's personal assistant for more than five years, and I always suspected that she felt that she had betrayed him when she left him to work with me.

"The last time I saw him was at my funeral," I said.

"That's the last time I saw him, too. I'm so glad we got the chance to talk. We went to dinner the night before your memorial service."

"What did you talk about?"

"About everything that happened between us. Good and bad. And we talked about you." She paused. "I finally got the chance to apologize."

"How did he respond to that?"

I think he used the word 'excruciating.' He said that my leaving, next to yours, was the most painful loss of his career, except he wasn't surprised that you left."

"Because I had no integrity?"

"No, because of your talent. He said he always knew that it was only a matter of time before you went off on your own. But I was one of those he never thought would leave."

"That must have been a little hard to hear."

"It was a lot hard to hear." She sniffed again. "But I needed to hear it. He said that through time he found peace with it. He understood the situation I was in and that I was not so different from him, seeking the bigger, better deal." Her voice temporarily lightened. "He also said that you could sell sand to an Arab, so it was understandable."

"I'll accept the blame," I said.

"No. I knew what I was doing. And, frankly, if I had to do it over, I would make the same decision again."

"Really?"

"It's been a roller coaster, Charles. Even now. I don't regret a second of it . . . and we never would have become the friends we are." She paused. "You're still my best friend."

Her words moved me. "You're my best friend, too," I said. I thought for a moment, then said, "Actually, you're my only friend, so that's a pretty low bar."

She laughed, which was comforting to hear. "Thanks for pointing that out."

"So, you didn't tell McKay that you would have done it again, did you?"

"No. There was no point. But I did accept responsibility for my choosing to go with you. It didn't feel right to blame it on you."

"I wouldn't have cared. I'm a dead man. At least you thought I was."

"I didn't want to speak ill of the dead."

"Loyal even after my death. That's impressive."

"Don't get too excited. I told him you were still an arrogant jerk."

I laughed. "Loyal *and* honest. So what did he say when you said that it was your decision?"

She laughed again. "He said 'It's just sewage under the bridge.'"

"Sounds like the McKay I knew."

"The thing is, it wasn't. He was a different McKay," she replied. "Facing death changes the paradigm. I'm glad I talked to him. I knew I had hurt him, but I didn't realize how much what I had done bothered me. I felt free."

"I know what you mean," I said. "Freedom from the chains of conscience. So, is there a funeral service?"

"It's Saturday."

"Where?"

"Near his home in Florida."

"Are you going?"

"Yes."

I thought for a moment, then said, "I think I will, too."

"You want to go to his funeral?"

"I think I owe him that. I mean, he went to mine."

"Isn't that . . . risky?"

"I'll wear a disguise. It worked before."

"That was at *your* funeral. No one was expecting to see you."

"They still aren't. Of course, there were only six people at my funeral."

"Seven," she corrected. "Actually, eight, counting you."

"Pathetic that I was more than ten percent of my audience," I said. "What airport are you flying into?"

"Fort Lauderdale. It's only four miles from Hollywood. Shall I book your flight?"

"Yes."

"From which airport?"

"LAX. Barstow's only a hundred miles from LA."

"When do you want to fly out?"

"Tomorrow."

"I'll check the flights and get back to you." She hung up, calling back only a few minutes later. "Friday morning there's a nine-fifteen direct flight out of LAX to Fort Lauderdale. It arrives at 5:09."

"Book it. And I'll need a room for Thursday night at the Hyatt Regency near LAX."

"Done. I'll text you the confirmation number. Do you think you'll have problems getting through security with your ID?"

"Why would I have trouble?" I asked.

"Because you're dead."

I hadn't thought about that. "I don't know. I read that

it takes upwards of six months for credit card companies to process a death. I can't imagine the government being faster. I guess we'll see."

"And if they stop you?"

"We'll go to plan B."

"What's plan B?"

"I'll walk."

She laughed. "I can always book you a private jet."

"As a last resort," I said. "When are you flying in?"

"Same day as you. My flight arrives about an hour earlier. I can wait for you."

"Where are you staying in Florida?"

"The Hollywood Beach Marriott. I'll book your room, too. Shall I book you a suite?"

"An ordinary room will do. Thank you."

"You're welcome." She was quiet a moment, then said, "Are you okay?"

"Yes."

"I mean, with McKay . . ."

"Ask me tomorrow. I'm sure it will sink in tonight."

"He forgave you, you know."

"I know."

She paused for a moment, then said, "It will be good to see you. I miss you."

"I miss you, too. I'll take you to dinner."

"I'll hold you to that," she said. "Good night."

"Ciao. Good night."

I lay back on my bed and spoke into the silence. "I'm sorry, McKay." I hoped he'd heard me.

Chapter Twenty-Three

Spending the night in a hotel Monica and I once happily shared only compounded the weight of loss on my heart.

CHARLES JAMES'S DIARY

I woke early the next morning but didn't get up. I just lay in bed thinking, preoccupied with McKay. I was grieving, I knew that, but there was something much more complex about my feelings. McKay's life, in a sense, was a foreshadowing of mine. We had once held the same ambitions, the same dreams, the same passions. When I first met him he was everything I wanted to be. And now he was gone. Everything he'd worked for was gone.

I went out to the pool and swam for an hour, then came back to my room and showered. I went downstairs and ate breakfast. I arranged for an Uber to pick me up at one, then went back up to my room and just lay there until the front desk called to see when I was checking out. I gathered my things and went down to the lobby to wait for my car.

My Uber driver drove a dated metallic-blue Toyota Camry. His name was Dale, and he looked to be in his mid-thirties. He had a slight beard and long hair.

After we had left Barstow I asked him, "How long have you been driving?"

"About six months."

"How's it working out?"

He tilted his head. "Not going to retire off it, but it's nice having a little extra. Winning in the margins, you know?"

"What's your day job?"

"I work for a company that seals concrete."

"Epoxy?"

"Same idea. It's an acrylic finish. We put it in garages, patios, walkways . . . pool decks. Protects it from chlorine, gas, salt, that kind of stuff."

"I had that epoxy on my home in Chicago."

"Yeah, that epoxy is nice stuff. I told my boss we should do it, but he's not interested."

"Why don't you do it on your own?"

"He'd fire me for working on the side."

"You're working on the side here."

"It's not competition."

"I hear you."

"We did the Ramada you're staying at. The whole deck area."

"It looked nice," I said. "How long does that take?"

"Not long. Half a day. It's not bad work, except when it's hot."

"Does it pay well?"

"I make about twenty-seven an hour plus benefits."

"Not bad," I said.

"My boss is raking it in. He drives a BMW."

"I have a BMW," I said. I'm not sure why.

"You're from Chicago?"

"Yes."

"What are you doing here?"

"I'm walking Route 66."

He glanced over as if ascertaining whether I was lying or not. "How come?"

"Because it's there."

He grinned. "I've lived my whole life on 66. Not in the same town."

"You're not from Barstow?"

"No. Flagstaff."

"I was there a few weeks ago. Nice town. What brought you to Barstow?"

"A girl."

"A girl," I said. "The things we do for women."

"You can say that again."

"Was she worth it?"

He flinched. "She ran off with another guy."

"Why?"

He looked offended. "What do you mean, why? What kind of question is that?"

"A relevant one," I said, the life coach in me coming out. I was used to putting people on the spot. I used to relish it. "You haven't asked yourself that?"

"What's there to ask? She met someone better."

"Better? What does that mean?"

He really looked annoyed now. "It means he made more money."

I looked at him. "You know that?"

"Yeah, he was, like, a lawyer."

"And that's a step up?"

"A lawyer versus a concrete sealer? You tell me."

"I already did," I said. "I'd take the concrete sealer every time. You know what they call a hundred lawyers at the bottom of the ocean?"

"No."

"A good start."

He laughed. "You got that right."

"You're processing this in the wrong way," I said.

"What do you mean?"

"You're processing this to hurt, not help you. You see, there's the thing that happened, and the thing we tell ourselves about what happened. They're not usually the same thing. It's about the narrative."

"So what's my narrative?"

"I'm guessing your narrative is that you're the victim here."

"Aren't I?"

"I don't know. But I wouldn't claim it if I were."

"Yeah? Then what would you call it?"

"There are two reasons she might have left you. First,

as you said, she met someone with more money. If that's the case, you owe that guy big-time, because he did you the biggest favor of your life."

"How's that?"

"He took the bullet for you. A woman who chooses her life mate by the thickness of his wallet instead of the quality of his character is someone all men should run from. You owe that man big-time."

"It still hurts."

"Detox always hurts," I said.

He thought a moment, then said, "You said there are two reasons she might have left. What's the other?"

"The other is because you really do suck."

He laughed. "That's blunt."

"Well, do you?"

He didn't respond. "I didn't hit her, if that's what you're asking."

"It's not," I said. "And that's a pretty low bar."

He didn't speak.

"So if she left you because you suck, she still did you a favor."

"How is that?"

"Because no one is happy living in a sick relationship, whether they're the weak link or the strong one. And if you're the weak link, this is your chance to learn that."

"What are you, a marriage counselor?"

"No. I'm a weak link."

He looked over. "Yeah?"

"I drove off the one woman who loved me, then spent

the rest of my life making excuses instead of owning up to what I did."

"That sucks."

"More than you can possibly imagine. . . ." My words trailed off in silence.

A few minutes later he said, "It's expensive to drive to LA. You could have taken a bus."

"Then what would you do?"

He grinned.

"Money's not really an object."

"That must be nice."

"It solves one problem," I said. "What do you do after you drop me off? Just turn around and head back?"

"No. Not in this traffic. I've got a buddy who lives in Venice. Do you know LA?"

"Yeah."

"It's just south of Santa Monica. Anyway, we're going to get dinner, then I'll go back in the morning."

We pulled up to the Marriott's porte cochere around four. There was a backup of cars waiting for the hotel valets, so I had Dale pull up to the curb and I got out, pulling my backpack from his car's backseat. I handed him a hundred-dollar tip. "Drive safe."

"Woah." He grinned at me. "Thanks, man. And thanks for the advice."

"For what it's worth," I said.

I walked inside the hotel. The lobby was a brilliant white with bronze pendant lights, marble floors, and dark wood trim. I had arrived at what was likely the peak check-in period, so even though every counter was occupied with a clerk, I still had a ten-minute wait before checking in to my room.

"I see it's not the first time you've stayed with us," the clerk said to me. "Welcome back."

"Thank you."

He handed me my room card. "Enjoy your stay."

Instead of going to my room, I went straight to the bar. I had stayed here at least half a dozen times before. Things had happened here. Back in 2006 I'd been here with McKay. I had been working for him for only a couple of months and was still intimidated by his presence. After a few drinks he'd asked me where I saw myself in five years, something he often asked from the stage. I'd responded with "Doing what you do." He'd taken a drink, then said, "Be careful what you wish for."

I'd also been here with Monica. We had met here once between shows. Santa Monica was only about fifteen miles from the hotel, and since I was leaving early the next morning it was easier for her to come to me. Besides, with McKay footing the bill, it was like an all-expenses-paid vacation.

It was my second year working for McKay, and I was finally starting to make some decent money. I remembered being excited that we could afford to eat at a real restaurant, something my own father had not been able to provide. I also remembered how beautiful Monica looked sitting across from me, her eyes reflecting the candlelight. She would get quiet at times like that, her usual vivacious self hidden beneath a layer of reflection. I remembered thinking that she was the most beautiful woman I had ever seen and how lucky I was to have her.

Monica had spent the night with me in the hotel. I remember we made love all night. A sad smile crossed my lips as I thought about it. It had been glorious. I drained my drink and ordered a second.

Chapter Twenty-Four

On my flight to Florida I sat next to a pastor who taught me something about forgiveness. In the Bible, the Hebrew word for repentance is shub, which literally means to turn around. Repentance is a change of heart—a spiritual U-turn, not punishment or penance.

CHARLES JAMES'S DIARY

I woke the next morning at a quarter past six to my alarm, and it took me a moment to remember where I was. It felt strange to have left the road. Like skipping ahead in a book.

I ordered eggs Benedict from room service, showered, ate breakfast, and then went downstairs to catch the shuttle to the airport.

The terminal was filled with its usual mass. I passed through the TSA checkpoint without a problem. I guess dead men can still fly. I picked up a copy of *USA Today* and a coffee, then went to my gate and read until they announced the preboarding of my flight.

My seat was in the first-class section. As I entered, I nodded to the man sitting in the chair next to mine. He was sipping a cranberry juice. He was large, his chest nearly as wide as the seat. I guessed he might have been in the military.

"Paul Roberts," he said, extending a massive hand.

"Charles Ja—" I stopped myself.

"Charles Jay," he said, his brow furrowing. "I knew some Jays. In Sacramento."

"Probably related somehow," I said quickly.

He finished drinking his juice, then said, "This is nice, sitting in first class. It's a first for me."

"Ever?"

He nodded. "It's too much of a luxury for my budget."

"A big man like you, it's more a necessity than a luxury."

"It's not important. I can take anything for a few hours. It only bothers me when the person next to me is large, too. Then it gets a bit uncomfortable. Or when I inconvenience someone. On my last flight I had the window seat, and the man in the aisle seat had at least fifty pounds on me. The woman sitting between us looked like she was trapped in a slot canyon. She must have held her breath the whole flight."

I laughed. "So how did you end up in first class?"

"It's all they had left, and I needed to get there tonight for a conference."

"What do you do?" I asked.

"I'm a pastor."

His declaration surprised me. "Didn't see that coming," I said. "Of what church?"

"A nondenominational Christian church," he said. "In Riverside. And what do you do?"

"I walk," I said.

"Like the apostle Paul," he said.

"Were you named after the apostle?" I asked.

"No. My parents weren't Christian."

"How long have you been Christian?"

"I was sixteen when I found God. Up until then, I thought I *was* God."

I thought of my own words, *There's no God but me.* I hadn't used the phrase for weeks. I just didn't feel it anymore.

"Are you a Christian?" he asked.

"I grew up a Catholic. So I was. Carried my Bible to school with me. But I left the faith about the same age you started."

"What happened?"

"My father beat it out of me."

He nodded sympathetically. "Not the first time I've heard that."

"What's it like being a pastor?"

"I enjoy it. It's a lot easier than being a Christian."

"What do you mean?"

"As a pastor, there's a certain expectation. Most people around me have similar beliefs. That's why they're around me. But as a Christian, you're on your own."

"What do you mean?" I asked again.

"For instance, my first day in college, my English professor asked, 'Do we have any Christians in the classroom?'

Out of a hundred of us, about twenty raised our hands. He said, 'We'll see how that goes.'

"Every day over the next quarter he would make snide comments about Christianity. Every now and then he and I would get into it. I was only eighteen at the time, but I was pretty passionate. The last day of class he said, 'How many of you are Christian? Stand up.' This time, only three of us stood. He looked at me and said, 'Roberts, I want to see you in my office after class.'

"Everyone looked at me with pity. I didn't know if he could fail me for being a Christian, but I was pretty sure he would if he could.

"After class I knocked on his office door. He said to come in. I walked in and he said, 'Shut the door.' He looked down for a moment, then said, 'Roberts, I want to apologize for all the crap I've put you through this quarter. There's a reason.' He actually teared up. He said, 'My life is a mess. My wife left me. My kids won't speak to me, and I'm alcoholic. I wanted to know if there were any real Christians left. I didn't want to trust anyone who wasn't at least willing to defend his faith.'"

"That's a good story," I said. "It's a hard time to be a Christian."

"It's always been a hard time," he said. "More Christians are being martyred today than in Roman times. Fortunately, Christianity isn't fragile."

"So, do you take confessions?"

"No. That's above my pay grade. That's God's job."

"Then what do you do when someone sins?"

"We all sin," he said. "I tell them what Jesus said."

"What's that?"

He grinned. "Stop sinning."

I laughed. "And confession?"

"That's between you and God."

"You don't believe in punishment?"

"Not from me," he said.

"Then what's repentance?"

"Repentance isn't about paying for our sins; that's what Christ did. It's about rethinking our actions. It's literally changing your mind. Punishment doesn't do that. Punishment can create obedience but not true changes of heart. And that's what God wants. Our hearts. If you want to know how well punishment and shame work, just look at our country's penal system."

I liked this guy. "Good luck with your conference," I said.

He smiled. "Good luck with your life."

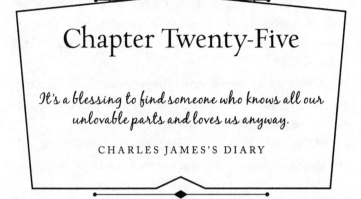

Chapter Twenty-Five

It's a blessing to find someone who knows all our unlovable parts and loves us anyway.

CHARLES JAMES'S DIARY

My flight touched down in Florida about twenty minutes before it was scheduled to arrive. I was feeling anxious about the funeral but glad to be seeing Amanda. She was waiting outside the Jetway door for me. She looked pretty. She was wearing a cheerful floral sundress. I don't know why I thought she'd be wearing black. She smiled when she saw me.

"There you are," she said. We hugged. "How was your flight?"

"Long," I said.

"Still faster than walking it. Did you check your backpack?"

"Yes."

"Baggage claim is this way." I followed her to the carousels. "How are we getting to the hotel?"

"I reserved a car." I retrieved my pack, and then we walked outside the terminal to the rental car lot. The temperature was not as warm as Barstow but the air was much more humid.

Amanda had already done the paperwork, and the car was waiting for us. She tossed me the keys to a Cadillac. I threw them back to her. "You drive."

"All right." We both climbed into the car. She started the engine. "How does it feel to be off the road?"

"Like halftime at the Super Bowl."

"What does that mean?"

"It means my body is beaten up, and the most important part is yet to come."

She smiled, then backed out of the stall. We drove toward the garage exit.

"I forgot where we're staying," I said.

"The Hollywood Beach Marriott. You've been there before. You liked it." She reached over and touched the navigation screen. "It's about half an hour from here."

"Have you spoken again with Marissa?"

"This morning."

"How was she?"

"She's a wreck. The boys aren't handling this well."

"How old are they?"

"Five and six. I can't imagine what Marissa's going through. Handling that much personal grief and trying to comfort her boys as well."

"She really loved him, didn't she?" I said.

Amanda glanced at me. "Of course. You sound surprised."

"You know, the whole trophy wife thing. You never know if it's real or . . . something else."

"She loved him. Loves him."

"This must be so confusing for those boys. Death is . . . confusing." I let out a short sigh. "Where is the service being held?"

"It's in Hollywood. Someplace called the DiSera Beard Chapel." She glanced at me again. "I was mistaken about the service. I thought it was a viewing, but McKay requested to be cremated."

"We talked about that once."

Amanda glanced over. "We did?"

"I meant McKay and me. One of his former associates had just died and had a fifteen-foot monument built for himself in the Orange County cemetery. They say you can't take it with you, but he tried. His casket was pure copper."

"What did that cost?"

"The whole service was more than a million."

"Think how many people he could have fed with that," Amanda said.

"Not that I have a right to criticize," I said. "I've spent plenty on my own self-aggrandizement. But at least I was around to see it, you know? After you're in the ground, why bother?"

Amanda looked at me with a pleased smile. "You've changed."

"I know. I've lost weight."

She grinned. "There's something else. Marissa told me McKay asked to have his ashes scattered at the top of Mount Elbert."

"Where's Mount Elbert?"

"It's the highest mountain in Colorado."

"McKay always loved the mountains in Colorado. I'm surprised he didn't want his ashes scattered in Vail."

"Then people would ski on him."

"They could put them in the trees."

"You haven't seen them ski in Vail," she said.

"So who's going to scatter his ashes on top of the mountain?"

"She has no idea. She's overwhelmed enough without that."

I thought a moment, then said, "Tell her you'll take care of it."

Amanda looked at me. "How am I going to do that? I get winded climbing the stairs."

"I didn't mean you're going to take them there. I'm going to do it. You just need to buy time for me to finish my walk."

"Far as I recall, you're not a mountain climber, either."

"I've just walked two thousand miles. I'm in the best shape of my life. I could climb Everest."

"No you couldn't."

"No, I couldn't, but I'm pretty sure this Elbert mountain isn't Everest. I'm sure I could climb it. As long as it doesn't require ropes."

"Or a Sherpa," she said.

"I could use a Sherpa."

She was quiet a moment, then looked at me. "Why do you want to do this?"

"McKay helped me climb my mountain. It's only appropriate that I return the favor."

She nodded. "I like that."

We arrived at the Marriott around seven thirty. Amanda checked us both in, then asked, "Are you hungry?"

"Famished."

"Me, too. The concierge says that there's a really good waterfront seafood restaurant about a mile from here."

"That sounds good. When did you talk to the concierge?"

"Before you landed. I'll have the concierge make us a reservation."

"All right."

"Can you give me twenty minutes to freshen up?"

"Take all the time you need."

"I'll ask them to make our reservations for eight. I'll meet you down here at . . ." She glanced at her watch. ". . . quarter to."

"You got it."

"And Charles . . ."

"Yes?"

"There will be a lot of McKay's associates in town. Don't forget your disguise."

"My own mother won't recognize me."

"That's not a good endorsement," she said. "Wait, I almost forgot something." She handed me two pill bottles. "You mentioned in Amarillo that you had a lot of body aches. I thought this might help. I had Dr. Cannon get it for me. Just don't overdo it; they're both super potent."

I looked at the labels. Fentanyl and OxyContin. "These are serious."

"I figured if Tylenol were enough, you would have already been using it. But only use them in case of severe pain. They're addictive."

"Thank you," I said.

"I've got your back," she said. She gave me a short hug, then walked to the elevator.

I put the pills in my pocket. "I'm glad someone does," I said.

Chapter Twenty-Six

Looking back over my life, I find that I, like everyone else, have colored my memories—some black and white, some sepia, and some in technicolor. I wonder in what other ways I've altered the film.

CHARLES JAMES'S DIARY

All I had in my backpack were T-shirts. I stopped in the boutique in the hotel lobby and purchased a Cubavera silk button-down bowling shirt that made me look like Charlie Sheen. I went up to my room to change. I combed my hair, put on my sunglasses, and then went back down to the lobby. My disguise worked better than I'd planned, since fifteen minutes later Amanda came out of the elevator and walked right past me.

She stood just a few yards from me looking around. I watched her in amusement. Then I spoke with my best Aussie accent, "'Scuse me, miss, could you direct me to the lift?"

She started to answer, then stopped herself. "How long have you been standing there?"

"I was here before you got here," I said. "You walked right past me."

"At least we know the disguise works."

"Should we walk?"

"It's a mile. At least."

"And that's a problem?"

"It is for me. You forget, we Americans don't walk. Maybe a block, but past that . . ."

I raised my hand. "Give me the valet ticket, I'll get the car."

The valet brought our car forward and I drove us to the restaurant, GG's Waterfront Bar & Grill. It was a beautiful clear night, and we drove with the windows down.

The lobby was crowded, and even though there appeared to be a long line to get in, we were seated almost immediately. The hostess led us to a table next to a window that was maybe a dozen feet from the water, offering a picture-perfect view of passing sailboats.

"There you are," the hostess said, handing us menus. "Table 4L. Enjoy your meal."

"Thank you," Amanda replied.

I took off my glasses and set them on the table. "Four-L?"

"The *Miami Herald* lists table 4L as the best seat in the house," Amanda said.

"I've forgotten how the other half lives," I said.

"I think that's changed to the other two percent," she said.

The restaurant was elegant, with parquet flooring

and linen-clad tables beneath beautiful chandeliers. The walls were lined with umber-stained wainscoting below porthole-like windows.

Our waitress walked up. "May I get you something to drink?"

"I'd like a lemon drop," Amanda said.

"Just a Coke," I said.

"Do you have any questions about the menu?"

"We haven't had a chance to look at it yet," I said.

"I'll get your drinks." She walked away.

"Where did you find that shirt?" Amanda asked. She knew all my clothes.

"I bought it in the hotel."

"You look like Charlie Sheen."

"I was going for that," I said. "I'll need to get some clothes for the service."

"I already took care of that."

"You did?"

"I stopped by your house and picked up a suit for you."

"Which one?"

"The Ermenegildo Zegna."

"That's the same one I wore to *my* funeral."

"That's appropriate. I hope it still fits you."

"Why do you say that?"

"You've changed body shape. Maybe I need to walk the Route, too."

"No, you don't." I looked at the menu. "What are you getting?"

She opened her menu. "I guess I'd better decide."

A few minutes later our waitress returned with our

drinks. Amanda ordered their cioppino with horseradish and maple Brussels sprouts. I ordered their stone crab claws to start, followed by twin lobster tails and a side of truffled mushrooms.

After our waitress left, Amanda took a drink of her cocktail and said, "I've been thinking; maybe I should stay in your house until you get back. Not that I'm a squatter. Just to protect it."

"That's a good idea."

"Think your neighbors will notice?"

"I don't think they know I'm dead yet."

"I'll move out before you get back."

"What will you bring over?"

"Just clothes."

"Just? You have a lot of clothes."

"Tons," she said. "And yet nothing to wear."

"The first-world dilemma. On the road I sometimes wear the same thing for three or four days."

"That's . . . disgusting."

"I don't have anyone to impress."

"What about yourself?"

"I'm past that. I know myself too well. At least I don't waste time deciding what to wear."

"That's exactly what time is for." Amanda took another sip of her cocktail and said, "Don't turn around."

"Which makes me want to turn around. What's behind me?"

"Two tables behind us. It's Marco, from Wealth Warriors."

I groaned. "Has he noticed you?"

"He would have been over here if he had. The last time I saw him he tried to get me back to his hotel room."

"The guy has a rep."

"A bad one."

I put my sunglasses back on. In the dim light it was hard to see. Marco never came over, which Amanda attributed to the amazing amount of alcohol he consumed. She was counting his drinks.

"I'm sure he didn't recognize me," she said. "If I were that sloshed, I wouldn't recognize my own mother."

"When was the last time you saw him?"

"Three or four years ago."

"Yeah. It's the booze."

We had ordered key lime pie and coconut flan for dessert but decided to take them with us.

Back at the hotel, we surrendered the car to the valet and I carried our desserts out back to the torchlit patio. The ocean was dark, barely visible through an inky haze, but still revealed by the loud crashing of waves on the beach.

"I love the ocean at night," I said. "It's terrifying."

"You love terrifying?"

"I love terrifying. There's no adventure without it."

She nodded thoughtfully. "Do you remember what you said to me the first time we met?"

"We were in Lincoln," I said.

"Tulsa."

"Right," I said, not really remembering where we were.

On the road I usually couldn't remember what city I was in, let alone where I'd been the day before. Once I got onstage and told everyone how much I loved Cleveland. Someone shouted from the first row, *That's great, but you're in Denver.* The truth was, I just knew better than to question her. She was always right about details like this.

"I don't remember."

"You asked me what it was like working for the greatest salesman on the planet."

I remembered. "You said, 'It's a privilege.'"

"Then you said, 'Someday I hope someone will say that about me.' I said, 'You hope that you're the world's greatest salesman?' And you said, 'No, I hope they say that it's a privilege to work for me.'"

"You must have thought I was crazy."

"I thought you were earnest. I didn't doubt that you would someday be the world's greatest salesman."

I looked at her. "Thank you."

"In case I've never told you, it's been a privilege."

Chapter Twenty-Seven

I met McKay's wife, Marissa, and her children. Marissa was lovely and broken, which are not incongruent. But the innocent boys' eyes haunted me with condemnation.

CHARLES JAMES'S DIARY

I woke early the next day, the morning sun stealing through the half-opened blinds, striping my room in gilded bars. I put on my shorts and a Meramec Caverns T-shirt, then went out the back of the hotel, off the property, and onto the long, pearl strip of coastline. The beach was quiet, the waves and gulls competing for airtime.

After half a mile I took off my shoes and walked along the beach where the sand was wet and hard, left bubbling by retreating waves and manic sand crabs. The sun was rising above the horizon, turning everything around me an iridescent rose gold. I suppose those who live on the East Coast come to expect this, but it was something I would never get tired of.

My heart hurt thinking about McKay's service and what Amanda had told me about his being cremated. Part of me wanted to see him again and feel that finality. The other half of my heart dreaded all of it—being forced to look into the face of mortality.

I suppose that's why the thought of carrying his ashes to the top of a mountain made me feel right, extending the end so I could have enough time to figure out what the end should be. It would be a last moment spent together. Just the two of us, like it had once been. At least it was something I could do for him and those he left behind.

I found that even with my disassociation from religion and my dubious profession of not believing in any god, my instinctual thoughts of life and death were still shaded by my childhood belief in an afterlife. I wondered where McKay was and what he was doing.

A peculiar thought crossed my mind. I wondered what he thought when he got to the other side and discovered that I wasn't there. I assumed they didn't do seminars on the other side. Maybe in hell they still did.

I walked for nearly an hour before returning to my hotel. The beach was still not crowded; just the early risers were there, a man in waders fishing in the surf and a few die-hard para-surfers.

When I got back to my room the light was flashing on my room phone. Amanda had left a message asking if I wanted to join her for breakfast in the hotel restaurant. I called her back.

"Am I too late?"

"Just poured the coffee," she said. "Come on down."

I found Amanda sitting near the front of the restaurant next to a window, the morning sun illuminating her along with her surroundings. She was sipping coffee. She smiled when she saw me. She always smiled when she saw me.

"Where have you been?" she asked.

"I went for a walk along the beach."

She shook her head in disbelief. "Really? You went for a walk?"

"It's what I do now. I didn't walk yesterday and I felt out of sync."

"How far did you walk?"

"Miles," I said. "So what's the plan?"

"The ceremony's at six. We should be there a little early."

I took a sip of my coffee. "Why?" I asked. "We've got nothing but time."

"That's not what I'm worried about."

"You're still worried someone will recognize me?"

"Yes."

A waitress came and took our orders. I ordered a Denver omelet.

"What are your plans today?" Amanda asked.

"Just the funeral. What about you?"

"I've got work."

"What work?"

"You think just because you died everything stopped?"

"I thought the world revolved around me."

"Nope. That's the sun."

"I'll have to pay you someday."

"That would be nice," she said.

After breakfast I went back to my room and took a long nap.

Even though we arrived before six, the parking lot was already full. The funeral home was nice but small, a far cry from the exorbitant Crystal Gardens, where my viewing had been held. Also unlike my viewing, there was a long line to get in.

Some of the people there were from Chicago. Tellingly, they had time to fly across the country for McKay's funeral but couldn't make it across town for mine.

For the first time I thought that Amanda was right and that coming might not have been such a good idea after all. Not only because it brought up painful memories but also because there was a very real chance that I might be exposed. Many of the people there I'd worked closely with. In the seminar world, backstage staff is a culture all its own. You learn to recognize people in the dark. Still, I felt uncomfortable wearing sunglasses.

"I want to take these off," I said.

"Don't," Amanda said. "Someone will recognize you."

"I look weird."

"You look like Bono."

"I look like Jim Jones."

"They'll just think you're mourning. Or you're Jim Jones. Either way they'll keep their distance."

The room was wide, with golden-brown carpet. Intricate, glossy white panels of wainscoting encircled the room. Marissa was standing near the front of the room next to a small shrine to McKay made up of framed pictures, awards, and a television monitor showing him speaking onstage. She was flanked by her two boys, who were huddled close together. An elderly man stood next to her, whom I guessed to be her father.

Suddenly a bear of a man walked up to us. I remembered him, not that I could have forgotten. His name was Mike Galbraith. He had been McKay's stage manager for the last five years I'd worked for him. The guy was a ruthless taskmaster, and everyone, except me, was afraid of him. He guarded stage time like the feds guard Fort Knox. If you were a minute over your allotted time, he'd be waiting for you in the wings to verbally share his displeasure, a wrath I'd evoked more than once.

The guy worshipped his facial hair. It was his defining characteristic. He talked about his beard in the third person. People would mention his beard and he would say things like, "There's a name for people without beards. Women." Or, "When people ask me if my beard is hot in the summer, I tell them, 'My beard is hot year-round.'"

Once, on the road, one of the stage crew showed up backstage wearing a shirt that read

FEAR THE BEARD

Galbraith liked it so much that he bought a T-shirt that read:

One Beard to Rule Them All

Mike and I never got along well, which I believed basically stemmed from the fact that he never realized that I was his superior. Still, he had a remarkable memory, and if anyone would recognize me, it would be him. Ironically, my beard was now longer than his. I turned slightly away from him.

"Panda!" he said gruffly. Panda was his contrived nickname for Amanda, a twisted compilation of her full name, Amanda Pike.

She turned and smiled at him. "I see you still haven't learned how to shave."

"Not in this lifetime. I'm like Samson. It's the source of my power."

I think he really believed that.

"It's good to see you, Mike," Amanda said.

"It's so good to see you, beautiful." He glanced furtively at me but otherwise didn't acknowledge me.

Amanda noticed. "This is Gabriel," she said. "My . . . boyfriend."

"Your boyfriend," he said, turning to me. "You have one of those now. I thought you were married to your work."

"I was."

"It's nice to meet you, Gabriel." For a moment he looked me over, then said, "Have we met?"

I shook my head. "No. I think I'd remember that beard."

He kept looking at me. "Are you sure? I never forget a face."

Amanda said, "He's never been around the circuit. I don't think he really even knows what I do. Or did."

"Good for him," he said. His brow furrowed. "No, I've met you. I never forget a face." He continued looking at me, and then suddenly his eyes brightened. "I know what it is. You look like Amanda's old boss, Charles James."

"You think?" Amanda said.

"I wouldn't know," I said.

"Wow, you even sound like him. Freaking doppelgänger," he said. "Take away the beard, add a few pounds, and you'd be the twin brother of the scoundrel."

"I'll take that as a compliment," I said.

"I wouldn't," he said. He turned back to Amanda. "Well, there you go. I never forget a face. So what are you doing now?"

"Floating, mostly. Just feeling my way through it."

"I bet. I could never get James off the stage, and then he makes this surprising midlife exit. So unexpected." He turned to me. "I'm sure you probably know, but her former boss was killed in a plane crash."

"I heard," I said.

"I worked with him for nearly ten years before he went off to do his own thing."

I almost corrected him but stopped myself.

"Where are you now, Mike?" Amanda asked.

"I'm with the Allen Finch Speakers Seminars," he said.

"And how's that going?"

"I like it. It's not as fiery as McKay's, but it pays the

bills. I'm positive I could get you on if you're interested. You were the best of the best."

"Thank you," Amanda said. "I don't know if I'm going to stay in this line of work. I'm keeping my options open."

"I'm glad you have that option," he said. "We're all meeting at the Social Room after to drink to McKay. Come join us." He obligatorily turned to me. "Both of you."

"Thank you," she said. "We might take you up on that."

"Well, carry on." He leaned forward and kissed Amanda on the cheek. "It's good to see you, Panda."

"You too, Mike."

He walked back to the group of men he'd been standing with. I recognized almost all of them, except now they all had beards.

"That was close," Amanda said.

"I still can't stand that guy."

"I know."

"Gabriel? My son?"

"It's just the first name that came to mind. Besides, I thought the boyfriend thing was the creative part."

"So are you going to meet up with the beards in the Social Room?" I asked.

"Not planning on it."

"You should. It'll be fun. All that facial hair."

She hit me.

It took us forty-five minutes to make it to the front of the line. As we neared it I couldn't take my eyes off McKay's boys. They were dressed sharply in matching suits with clip-on ties. They looked sad and dazed.

I couldn't guess how emotionally overwhelming it must have been for them. How difficult it would be to grow up never knowing their own father.

As I thought about this, the thought pierced me so deeply I could barely breathe. It was exactly what I had done to my own son. Only McKay's exit wasn't voluntary.

It may have been the first time I'd truly allowed myself to face what I'd done. What I was still doing. The extent of my feelings must have been visible, because Amanda took my arm. "Are you okay?"

I shook my head. "No. But I'll be okay."

Amanda looked doubtful but didn't press. "It will probably be easier on her if it's not obvious we're together," she said.

I nodded.

Marissa finished talking to a man who, as I gathered from their conversation, maintained their yacht. Afterward she looked over at Amanda and her expression relaxed into a soft vulnerability. She was clearly relieved to see her.

"Amanda," she said. The two women embraced. "Thank you for coming. It's so far."

"Of course I came," she said. "I'm so sorry, honey. I really am sorry."

"Thank you. McKay loved you."

A tear rolled down Amanda's cheek. "Is there anything I can do for you?"

"No. They tell me the hardest time is right after the funeral."

"How are the boys doing?"

"Not well. Little Marc keeps asking for his daddy."

Amanda wiped away another tear. "I'm sorry. I wish I could help more."

"We just have to muddle through it."

They embraced once more, and then Amanda glanced back at me, then away. Marissa looked at me, clearly not knowing who I was. We had never met. She looked exhausted. "I'm very sorry for your loss," I said.

"Thank you."

"He was a good man. We . . ." I stopped myself from elaborating. "I met him many years ago."

"You were friends?"

"Yes. In a different life."

"I'm sure he must have told me about you. What is your name?"

"Gabriel," I said.

She thought for a moment, then said, "I'm sorry, I don't remember. But thank you for coming."

I looked down at the boys. "How are you all holding up?"

"We're hurting."

I wanted to hug her. "Blessings to you all."

"To you, too."

I stepped past her. Amanda was standing at the far side of the room watching. I walked up to her. "Let's get out of here."

As we walked out to our car, the line was still outside the building. If anything, it was longer. Amanda was quiet.

After I pulled out into the street, Amanda said, "She didn't look well."

"No."

"I forgot to tell her about the ashes. I'll call her tomorrow. I was planning on calling her tomorrow anyway."

"Let me know what she says."

We drove a moment in silence. Then Amanda sighed. "Back to it." She looked over at me. "We need to talk sometime about work."

"What's going on?"

"I'm not sure what I'm supposed to be doing. Should I be keeping things alive or killing them?"

"What things?"

"Our office lease, to start. And our venue contracts. I've been canceling venues, but we have them two years out. Should I let them all go?"

I thought a moment. "I really don't know. I don't know what I'm going to do after I finish. I guess it depends."

"On what?"

"If Monica wants me."

It was the first time I'd been that honest since I'd started my walk. I don't think Amanda knew what to say. We dropped the subject.

As we pulled into the hotel's driveway, Amanda said, "You've got an early flight. You should leave for the airport before six. Sundays get slammed."

"What time is your flight?" I asked.

"Not until noon."

"I'll take an Uber."

"I'll drive you," she said. "Who knows how long it will be before I see you again?"

"Not too long," I said. "I only have a hundred and thirty miles left."

"Are you ready to be done?"

I slowly shook my head. "I don't know." I pulled up to the valet stand and we got out. As we walked into the hotel, Amanda said, "Want to get a drink?"

"No. I'm sorry. I think I need to be alone."

She looked at me, then said, "That affected you more than you thought it would, didn't it?"

I nodded. "Yes."

"Guilt?"

"More like shame. But not about McKay."

She cocked her head. "Then about who?"

"My son. I always thought my own father was a monster. I might be worse." I shook my head. "How could I have done what I've done?"

Chapter Twenty-Eight

I'm convinced that Amanda forgets nothing. What an awful curse. There are far too many things I'd pay dearly to forget.

CHARLES JAMES'S DIARY

I had a drink in my room. Then another. And another. I went to sleep with a buzz. That night I had a bizarre dream. I was back in the funeral home's chapel, only this time there was a casket. I wasn't alone. One of McKay's sons stood next to the casket, his back to me. I walked up to him. "I'm sorry," I said. But when the boy turned around, it was me. "Why did you leave me?" he asked.

I woke soaked in sweat. My head was throbbing. I went to the bathroom, wiped myself down with a towel, and then went back to bed.

I woke the next morning to the buzz of the alarm clock. I wanted to smash it and go back to sleep. I felt hungover, physically *and* emotionally.

I took a quick shower, put my dirty clothes in my pack, and then went downstairs to the lobby.

Amanda was already there waiting for me, wearing black Lycra exercise clothing.

"You're going to exercise after you drop me off?" I asked.

"I already did," she said. "I just finished."

"It's not even six. You're crazy."

"That's high praise coming from the Mad Hatter," she said. "Besides, the calories don't come off as easily as they used to."

We walked out to our car. The valet handed me the key, and I got in.

"You sure you don't want me to drive?" Amanda asked.

"The last time you drove me to the airport the plane crashed."

"Really? You're somehow connecting that tragedy to my driving?"

"I'm not saying that your driving had anything to do with that; I'm just pointing out a fact."

"No, you're implying culpability, and it's not a fact. You drove to the airport that day. You always drive."

"You remember that?"

"I remember everything. It's my curse. I can tell you what socks you were wearing that day."

"That's terrifying. I bet you could still tell me McKay's phone number."

"Which phone?" she said. "He had three."

I shook my head. "I'm still driving."

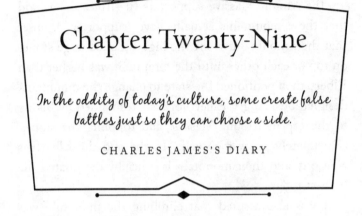

Chapter Twenty-Nine

In the oddity of today's culture, some create false battles just so they can choose a side.

CHARLES JAMES'S DIARY

My flight was delayed an hour, which, other than the boredom of sitting in the airport, didn't matter much. Either way I would get back to Barstow too late to start walking.

It was a long flight to California, but I had a lot on my mind. I landed at LAX and took an Uber back to Barstow, stopping along the way for dinner, which I bought for my driver at well. He was from India, and he showed me his favorite Indian restaurant. We arrived in Barstow at eight. I booked a room in the same Ramada.

That night I looked up Mount Elbert on my phone to see what I was up against. I learned that there was a bizarre competition going on between Elbert and Mount Massive, the second-tallest mountain in Colorado. Apparently Mount Elbert, at 14,439 feet, is only ten feet higher than Massive.

The Mount Massive supporters (it strikes me as odd that these mountains actually have "supporters"), upset that their mountain wasn't the highest, piled large stones on top of each other until the mountain was higher than Elbert, then petitioned the state to change the mountains' designations. Angry Elbert loyalists responded by hiking to the top of Mount Massive and toppling the stones. (Fortunately, no war ensued.) In the end the Elbertists won out, and their mountain is officially designated the highest today.

I was also assured that climbing the mountain was something I could do, since way back in 1949, someone drove a jeep to Elbert's summit.

Chapter Thirty

I feel like Frodo in Tolkien's Lord of the Rings trilogy—his errand more difficult, each footstep heavier, as he nears his destination.

CHARLES JAMES'S DIARY

Back to the road. Walking now felt like the final refrain of an interminable symphony. I walked through the towns of Lenwood and Hodge and spent the night in Helendale at the Silver Lakes Vacation Club.

The next morning I had breakfast at Molly Brown's Café, then, just a mile and a half later, came to Elmer's Bottle Tree Ranch, another cleverly contrived amusement designed to glean ducats from 66.

It's worth looking up if not visiting. Elmer Long, the bearded artist who designed the site, created an entire forest of trees made from colorful antique bottles attached by rods to vertical poles. Elmer and his father had spent their lives scavenging antiques, and there were myriad other artifacts throughout the bottle-tree forest, including old typewriters, milk cans, saw blades, old signs, gas pumps, mining equipment, and hundreds of other vintage curiosities.

Unfortunately, Elmer wasn't there, so I did a quick walk-through of the place, dropped a ten-dollar donation in the wishing well, and got on my way.

I stopped at the Iron Hog Saloon for a cola, then stopped again just an hour later in the city of Oro Grande for lunch. Forty-five minutes later I entered Victorville, crossing the Mojave River on a steel-truss bridge built back in the 1930s.

It seemed to me that there were a lot of homeless people in Victorville, and it made me think of cowboy Eric in Albuquerque and his homeless tribe. I spent the night at the Green Tree Inn.

The next morning I reached the town of Hesperia. I passed a sign I thought was a Route 66 designation but turned out to be a mileage sign informing me that it was just 66 miles to Los Angeles. If I were in a car, I'd be there in less than an hour.

The smooth, black road lowered into a long valley, and for once the temperature was cool, the sun shielded by the towering trees. I enjoyed it while I could. For most of the way the original, unrestored 66 ran parallel to the road.

I stopped at the Mitla Café for dinner. My surroundings reminded me of the California I knew, the streets lined with palm trees. I turned from Fifth Street onto Foothill Boulevard, a road I was familiar with from my time in Santa Monica. I spent the night at the Wigwam Hotel.

I got up at sunrise, stopping for breakfast at Yum Yum Doughnuts, then went back to heavy city walking, with traffic lights slowing my usual pace.

A little after noon I reached the town of Cucamonga. Maybe it was my fear of completion and its aftermath, but I suddenly decided that I was in no hurry and booked a room at the Doubletree along with a hot-stone massage and a much-needed pedicure.

I had planned to have dinner in their hotel restaurant when I walked past a banner for a Millionaire Mentor Seminar, a company started by one of my previous co-workers, which meant the hotel was likely crawling with former clients. So I spent the night in my room eating a steak and lobster dinner from room service.

The next morning I reached the city of Glendora in less than an hour, and Foothill changed to Colorado Boulevard. I passed the Santa Anita Racetrack and the Los Angeles County Arboretum in Arcadia. This was very familiar territory. Back when I did landscaping, we had two clients in Arcadia and one in neighboring Pasadena.

In spite of the difficulty of city walking, I made eighteen miles and spent the night just a little west of Rosemead at the Best Western Pasadena.

One more day to go.

Chapter Thirty-One

Kalah. I have finished my walk.

CHARLES JAMES'S DIARY

I woke the next morning with the heavy realization that this was the last day of my walk. From Pasadena I walked south on SR110—the Arroyo Seco Parkway—to Sunset Boulevard, then onto Santa Monica Boulevard. This was the most luxurious segment of my walk, and the traffic changed, not so much in quantity as in quality. I was being passed by a better class of cars—Rolls-Royces, Ferraris, and McLarens.

I was also only a few miles from our old home. I mused that it was possible that Monica might have even driven past me—not that she would have recognized me. I hardly recognized myself. But it was amusing to imagine her thinking, *That homeless guy looks a lot like my ex-husband.*

The original ending of Route 66 was in downtown Los Angeles at the intersection of Seventh and Broadway. But a decade after the creation of the Route, the terminus was moved to Santa Monica and the intersection of Lincoln and Olympic, which, even in heavy traffic, I reached by late afternoon.

The end of Route 66 is remarkably anticlimactic, quietly announced by a whisper of a sign mounted on the corner of Olympic and Lincoln Boulevards. The sign is just the usual small brown Route 66 sign with one variation—a small, rectangular addition below it that says END. That's it. After all that way I expected a more spectacular finale.

Apparently I was not the only one in America who felt that way, which is why a larger sign was erected on Santa Monica Pier, one that people would wait in line to have their picture taken next to and that, if not the official terminus, was definitely the more popular one.

From the route's finale I continued west down Olympic toward the Pacific Ocean and Santa Monica Pier.

Ten minutes later I saw the pier's carousel and its iconic landmark entrance, a large neon sign that read:

SANTA MONICA

YACHT HARBOR

SPORT FISHING • BOATING

CAFES

As usual, the pier was crowded with tourists both local and not. I crossed Ocean Avenue and walked up to the entrance, falling in with a flock of high school kids wearing gold-and-black Cottonwood High Marching Band T-shirts.

The sound of blended music—everything from the eclectic vibe of house to archaic Wurlitzer organs—created a cacophony as unique as the pier's collection of humanity.

Fifty yards from the pier's entrance I saw it—a twelve-foot-tall sign just north of the Pier Burger.

SANTA MONICA

66

END OF THE TRAIL

The emotion of reaching my destination surged powerfully through me. I wanted to shout out, but everyone would just think I was crazy.

I walked over to the north side of the pier and looked out over the white sand beach and its hundreds of bathers.

"I made it," I said to myself. "I walked Route 66."

For the first time since I left Chicago, my feet hurt.

Chapter Thirty-Two

*As afraid as I was to see my wife,
I was in no way prepared for what
was actually to transpire.*

CHARLES JAMES'S DIARY

Monica and I had spent many hours on the pier. In the early years of our marriage it was a cheap date, walking hand in hand sharing a funnel cake, or, if we felt rich, eating dinner at one of the restaurants.

It was a beautiful, sunny day. The usual panhandlers and rockers were there, one guy playing the drums to a recorded album. A plane flew overhead pulling a banner that read

CANNABIS DELIVERED

California, I thought. There was a family rock band with five members. The lead singer and guitarist was probably seventeen at the oldest. They all had hair that fell a half foot past their shoulders. They called themselves Liliac.

Next to them was a leather-clad futuristic dancer named Boris. I watched them both for a while, then walked off to a quieter section of the pier where a group of people were fishing.

I made it. It was almost painful to have accomplished such an amazing feat and have no one to tell. Oddly, the one I wanted to call first was Monica. That would have been frightening to her in more ways than one.

Then I thought of calling Jennifer, my shrink in Chicago, since it had been her advice to walk the route. Not the whole route, of course. I almost called her. In fact, I dialed her office number before remembering that she thought I was dead.

I ended up calling Amanda. She answered on the first ring.

"I'm here," I said. "I did it."

"You talked to Monica?"

"No. I made it to the end of Route 66."

"Congratulations. That's amazing. Now what?"

"I'm tired," I said. "I'm going to have a nice meal, in a nice hotel, and soak in a tub."

"May I book you a room at the Four Seasons Beverly Hills?"

"That would be perfect."

"I wish I were there to celebrate with you."

I looked around the crowded pier. "So do I."

"I'll call the hotel and text you the confirmation."

"Remember, Beverly only has two *e*'s in it."

"Thanks," she said, a smile in her voice. "Congratulations, Charles."

I put the phone back in my pocket and headed toward the entrance to the pier. On my way out I stopped, for old times' sake, for a funnel cake with strawberries and whipped cream, then sat on a fence rail to eat.

I finished the funnel cake, then headed toward the parking lot where the taxi drivers were lined up. "Beverly Hills Four Seasons," I said, climbing into a bright-green cab.

"The Four Seasons on Doheny Drive," the driver replied, nodding. "We'll be right there."

As we pulled out of the pier's parking lot, it occurred to me that everything was different now. It was like graduation. It was time to find a new life.

The lobby of the Four Seasons was as opulent as anything I'd experienced since I left Chicago. Considering how I was dressed, I felt out of place, like a drifter, and I noticed that the bell captain gave me a reserved, sideways glance as I walked past him into the marble-floored foyer.

I gave the clerk at the registration desk my ID, and she smiled and said, "It's good to have you back, Mr. James. We have your card on file. Everything is taken care of. I have you on the eleventh floor. Is there anything else I can do for you?"

"Not now, thank you. It's just good to be back."

"Have a pleasant stay."

I picked up my backpack and took the elevator up to

my room. There was a bottle of Dom Pérignon on the counter with a handwritten note from the management.

Congratulations on finishing your walk.

Amanda, I thought. The message light was flashing on my phone. I lifted the receiver and pushed the button.

"Mr. James, I'm Sally, the concierge. I'm just calling to welcome you to the Four Seasons and let you know that your sixty-minute massage appointment is scheduled for three thirty p.m. The spa advises that you arrive at least fifteen minutes early for check-in. If there is anything else I can do for you, please don't hesitate to call. Have a good evening."

It was a little past three when I took the elevator down to the fourth-floor spa, where I put on a robe and slippers and drank chamomile tea to ambient nature sounds—a combination designed to bring on a state of relaxation. Unfortunately, it didn't take. There was too much Monica on my mind.

My masseuse, a svelte young blond woman named Candace, commented on my muscle tone. "I've never seen legs that muscular," she said, rubbing lavender oil into my calves. "I'm jealous. What's your secret? Stair-Master?"

"Something like that," I said. I wasn't in the mood to talk. The truth was, I wasn't really even in the mood for a massage. I felt like I was a few hours away from the biggest audition of my life—one I was destined to fail.

I had celebrated the completion of my walk too soon.

My destination wasn't the Pacific, my destination was *her*. And now I wished that I still had a thousand miles to go. Still, I knew that I couldn't delay seeing her any longer. For better or worse, it was time to face the truth.

I thanked Candace with a large tip, got dressed, and then went back up to my room. I lay down on my bed for a few minutes, then got up and looked through the in-room dining menu. I even picked up the phone to order room service, but stopped myself. I wasn't hungry. I was avoiding. It was time to man up.

I was fiercely tempted to have a drink to calm my nerves, but decided against it. I had to have all my faculties. And the last thing I needed was for Monica to smell liquor on my breath and think that I'd been drinking.

I put on the shirt I'd bought for McKay's funeral, then went down to the hotel entrance. The bell captain hailed me a taxi.

"Where are we going?" the driver asked.

"Santa Monica. Winnett Place."

"That's the name of the street?"

"Yes."

"Hold on, please. Let me put that in my navigator," he said, lifting his phone. "Winnett. W-i-n-e—"

"W-i-n-n-e-t-t," I corrected. "Just take San Vincent Boulevard west."

"Thank you."

"I'll need you to wait for me and bring me back."

"No problem," he said. He pulled out of the hotel's driveway. The traffic seemed lighter than usual, not nearly as congested as my thoughts. I didn't want the traffic to be light. I wanted more time. The truth was, I was scared. I had stood on stages before audiences of thousands without a twinge of nerves. But I was terrified to stand on this stage before an audience of one. I was asking for something more than mere money. More, even, than forgiveness. I was asking her, a newly engaged woman, to love me again.

The absurdity of that made my heart and stomach ache. How had that not been apparent to me over the last two thousand miles? Then add to that the fact that I was supposed to be dead . . .

Driving into the old neighborhood brought back a flood of memories. Everything looked older—more grown, more worn. Like me. The neighbor who used to play Grateful Dead music every Sunday as he washed his metallic-green dune buggy still lived there. Or at least the dune buggy still did. It looked ancient, too.

As we turned onto Winnett, I said to the driver, "It's the olive-trimmed house up ahead. Right there."

"Got it," the driver said. A moment later he pulled up to the curb in front of my old home. The brick wall in front of the house was now covered with ivy; the bougainvillea plants I'd planted as saplings near them were now large and spilling over the wall in a cascade of brilliant purple. "You want me to wait, sir?"

"Yes."

"How long do you think you'll be?"

"I have no idea. Could be an hour. Could be two minutes."

"It's thirty-two dollars an hour waiting."

"Don't worry about it," I said. I climbed out of the car and walked toward the driveway that was flanked by two redbrick pilasters.

There was no car in the driveway. As I walked up the driveway, I watched for someone to look out the window at me, but thankfully no one did. There was a boy's bicycle in the middle of the walkway, which I stepped over.

Bicycle aside, this was déjà vu. How many times had I bounded up this walkway, excited about the future that was rolling out in front of us?

I stopped at the base of the porch. The door was Creamsicle orange. Orange was Monica's favorite color. I couldn't remember what color the door used to be. Blue? *Why am I thinking about the color of the door?*

I knew why. It was a way of protecting myself from the reality of the moment, focusing on the most trivial of things, the color of the repainted door or the massive boxwood hedge we planted just after we'd moved in.

Standing in front of the door was like standing on the edge of the Grand Canyon without a guardrail. I must have stood there for at least ten minutes before climbing the two steps to the front porch. I reached over to ring the doorbell, then stopped. I knocked twice on the door.

Nothing. Maybe, after all that, they weren't even home. I glanced over at the driveway. It would be awful to have her drive up, I thought. I was considering walking away when I heard the doorknob shake. Whoever was on the other side seemed to be struggling with it.

Finally I heard a sharp click, and my heart froze. Honestly, I wanted to run. Then the door opened.

There stood a boy, his dark, tousled hair falling over his brow. My son.

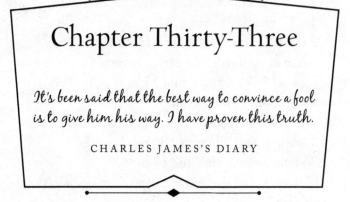

Chapter Thirty-Three

It's been said that the best way to convince a fool is to give him his way. I have proven this truth.

CHARLES JAMES'S DIARY

He looked like me. At least, what I remembered of the pictures I'd seen of myself as a boy. He looked at me with big, curious eyes. "Who are you?"

"I'm a friend of your mother's. Is she here?"

He shook his head. "She went to the store."

"Who's watching you?"

"Pam. She's my sitter."

Just then a woman in her mid-twenties walked up behind him. "May I help you?"

"I . . ." I hesitated. Then I said, "I'm a friend of Monica's. An old friend."

"Oh. I'm sorry, she's not here right now."

"That's what I was told," I said. I looked down at Gabriel, then back up. "I hear she's getting married."

The sitter nodded. "The end of next month."

"I've forgotten his name."

"Jay," she said. "Jay Stark."

"I think I know him," I lied. "He's a pediatrician."

Her eyes squinted. "No. He's a lawyer."

"I guess I don't know him," I said softly. "Have you been with Monica for a while?"

"Almost seven years."

"Good," I said. "How well do you know Jay?"

"Who are you again?" she asked.

"I'm sorry. I'm just an old friend from Idaho. Mountain Home."

She relaxed some. "Oh, right. Her father used to live up there on the army base."

I looked into her eyes. "Is he a good guy?"

"Her father?"

"No. The man's she's marrying."

"Oh," she said, shaking her head. "He's a good guy." She squinted a little. "You know, you look familiar. Have we met?"

"I don't think so."

"I'm pretty sure I've seen you before. Maybe Monica has a picture of you. It'll come to me."

"Do you want to come in?" Gabriel asked. "We're making cinnamon toast. Then we're going to play a video game."

The sitter smiled. "He's rather precocious for his age."

"Takes after his mother." I squatted down until I was at the same level as my son. "Thank you. But I better not." Suddenly a lump rose in my chest. "I should go." I just looked at him. What a beautiful boy. I fought back the emotion rising in my chest. My mouth was dry. How had I betrayed this beautiful, innocent little boy? My eyes began to well up. I needed to leave. "Be a good man," I said softly.

I stood back up and looked at the woman. "Did you hear that Monica's ex-husband was killed in a plane crash?"

"Yes."

"Did Monica cry?"

Her brow furrowed. "Did she cry?"

"I know it's a strange question, but it's important."

She thought for a moment, then said, "When I first met her, she cried a lot. Her ex was kind of a sleazebag. But that was a long time ago." She hesitated a moment, then said, "I don't think she cried. Not that I saw."

I swallowed. Then I looked back down into Gabriel's face. I rubbed his hair. "Take good care of him," I said to Pam.

I turned and walked away. My knees felt weak. I wanted to fall on them. I hadn't just walked 2,500 miles for nothing. I had lived for nothing.

Chapter Thirty-Four

My life, like my walk, has all been in vain.

CHARLES JAMES'S DIARY

"How did your meeting go?" my driver asked as I climbed into the backseat of the car.

"Back to the hotel," I said.

He glanced up at me in the rearview mirror, then started the taxi. "Yes, sir."

On the drive back I just looked out the window, my vision clouded by my thoughts. Or my tears. I couldn't get Gabriel's dark, piercing eyes out of my head.

The taxi pulled up to the hotel's front door. I tossed the driver a hundred-dollar bill and got out of the car, hurrying past the boisterous crowd in the hotel lobby. In the last three months I had walked alone through hundreds of miles of deserts, but I had never really felt alone until now. I went to my room and double-locked the door.

I needed something to dull the pain. I looked at the unopened bottle of Dom Pérignon. Not strong enough.

I opened the refrigerator and took out three bottles: two mini bottles of Jack Daniel's and one Beefeater gin. I immediately put down one of the whiskeys, burning my throat but only briefly distracting me from my pain. Tears began to fall down my cheeks. Then I downed the second bottle. Then I drank the gin.

I lay back on my bed as my head began to spin. *Take it away*, I thought. *Take him away.* But every time I shut my eyes he was still there. My son. His eyes locked on mine. If it wasn't him, it was McKay's two boys, huddled together at the funeral.

I went to the fridge and took out another bottle, this one vodka.

Why did I desert him? What had I sold him out for? Even with Monica divorcing me, I still could have been there. I had rationalized that a monthly check was *child support*. But that wasn't the support he needed most. My son needed me. His father. My *son*. How could I call him my *son*? The only thing that made him mine was my DNA.

I remembered the dream I had had in Florida of the little boy standing in front of the coffin, then turning to me and asking why I had left him. I thought it had been me I'd seen as a boy. But it wasn't. It was Gabriel. Only in seeing him in real life did I realize how much he looked like me.

Maybe what was fueling my pain the most was that, like Gabriel, I knew the pain of a father's rejection. I knew how much my son needed me, and still I had done this. In this way I had betrayed myself as well. That little boy was trying to navigate life in spite of a father who had abandoned him, just as I had tried to survive with a father who hated me.

It was then that, for the first time, I realized that I hadn't just lost Monica, my pearl, but everything of value in my life. And that all the money and fame I'd acquired couldn't buy it back. I had spent the last decade of my life trading diamonds for stones. What could be more painful than to finally know that one had lived for all the wrong things?

To look at yourself in the mirror of introspection and find yourself wanting. *Maybe this is hell*, I thought. Clarity. This was definitely hell.

Why am I still alive? Of all the lives that might have been spared in the plane crash, why was mine? I deserved it so little. I had ruined lives. I had driven people to suicide—I knew this. The tortured eyes of the heartbroken father in my office telling me about his son who had hanged himself still haunted me. And that's just the one I was confronted with. How many deaths had I contributed to? In the economy of the human cooperative, I didn't deserve to live.

Then why didn't I die in that plane crash? No, that's not what I was thinking right then. I was wondering why *couldn't* I have died in that crash. It was more my right to die than anyone else's on that plane. How many of them had so much more to live for—so much more to contribute to the world. So many more people who would truly mourn their deaths. I knew how many people were mourning my death. I could count them on one hand.

The emotional pain was searing. More, even, than

when I was nearly beaten to death by my father. I wanted out. I wanted to end my life. *Why shouldn't I?* Fate had cheated me out of my death, but that didn't mean I had to accept its verdict. I had the means. I had enough painkillers in my bag to end my pain.

I went to my pack and took out the two medicine bottles Amanda had given me. The drugs would work. And it was better than jumping out of an eleventh-story window. Less traumatic all around.

I wished that the bikers hadn't taken my gun. A bullet through my head would have made a more appropriate statement about the hate I felt toward myself. But the pills would work. Quietly, but just as final. A T. S. Eliot quote went through my head (instead of a bullet): *This is the way the world ends, not with a bang, but a whimper*. A whimper indeed.

I wondered how my body would respond to the drugs. Would it be painful? Would I suffocate or convulse, or would I just drift off to Neverland? I hoped for the latter, but the pain would work, too.

Amanda had gotten the pills to stop my pain. That's what I was using them for. She would blame herself for her part in this. I didn't like that, but not enough to let it hinder my resolve.

"Here it goes, God," I said out loud. "If you want me here, it's your last chance."

I opened the Dom Pérignon (I'm not sure how I accomplished this in my state) and began drinking from the bottle. Then I took the lids off both pill bottles and poured them into my hand. My head was spinning. This was it. There was no turning back.

I lifted my hand to my mouth, the blue and yellow pills mixed together. Then, in the quagmire of my muddled thoughts, a voice spoke—an external voice with an authority outside my own.

There's a reason you didn't die on that plane.

I looked around to see who had spoken to me. Then I dropped my hand and fell over and sobbed until I passed out.

Chapter Thirty-Five

I hadn't the courage or the stupidity to end my life. But suicide or not, the result is the same. I have killed my old self.

CHARLES JAMES'S DIARY

I woke the next morning lying on the floor. I didn't remember how I got there. At first I didn't even remember where I was. Pills were scattered around me, as were empty mini booze bottles. There was vomit as well. I could smell it before I saw it. My head was throbbing. Buzzing. So was my phone. "Who is it?" I mumbled, which was a foolish question. I got up on my knees, wiping drool and vomit from my mouth.

I stumbled over to the refrigerator. I was surprised at how many of the liquor bottles were gone. More than I remembered drinking. Had I really drunk that much?

I took out an energy shot from the mini fridge and drank it. Then I drank a second. My mind woke. I went into the bathroom and put a cold washcloth on my head, then walked back out. A minute later I ran back into the bathroom and vomited. I had never felt that hungover before. I got a cold can of ginger ale from the fridge, then lay back on the bed, holding the can to my forehead.

You almost killed yourself, I thought.

But I hadn't. Something had stopped me. A voice? Had I really heard a voice? *A guardian angel? God?* Or was I just drunk and the voice had spilled out of my unguarded subconscious? But even that had merit. It meant that something inside me still wanted to live, and that, too, was miraculous.

Whatever its source, the message was clear. *There was a reason I hadn't died on that plane.*

So what was that reason? What did I have to offer? At that moment a new intelligence entered my thoughts. There were things I could still do. Maybe I couldn't erase my own wrongs, but that didn't mean I couldn't erase *any* wrongs.

There's a reason you didn't die on that plane.

That would be my new motto. It would be my new reason to live. Suddenly a list of unfinished business ran through my mind. There were things I needed to set straight. I couldn't fix my life, but there were other lives I could fix. People who deserved it more than I did.

I picked up my phone and called Amanda.

"How are you?" she asked, her voice laced with concern.

"Hungover."

"How much did you drink?"

"Most of it," I said.

She hesitated. "Did you see Monica?"

"No," I said, rubbing a hand over my face. "I saw Gabriel."

"Oh."

"I mean, what did I expect? That walking two thousand miles would change the last eight years?"

"It has changed you," she said.

"It doesn't change the truth that they're better off without me."

"I don't think that's truth," she said. "Gabriel's not through living. He still needs you."

"Maybe eight years ago he did. Maybe even three years ago. But not now."

She was quiet for a moment, then asked, "Did you find out who Monica's marrying?"

"Yes. The sitter said he's a good guy. A lawyer. Maybe that's an oxymoron."

Amanda sniffed.

"She's found love," I said. "She deserves that. She can do better than me."

"That would be hard," Amanda said. We both were quiet for what felt like a full minute. I held the cold can back up to my forehead. Amanda asked, "So now what?"

"I've got some things I need to do before I go back to life."

"What kinds of things?"

"I want to set some things right."

"What can I do to help?"

"First, I need you to call Mumford."

"Your real estate agent?"

"Yes. There's a property I'm interested in purchasing in New Mexico."

"I'll get right on it. What else?"

"I haven't checked my email for a while. Will you go back and see if you can find an email from a man named Eddie De La Cruz? He's the migrant worker who helped me in Plainview."

"Do you know his email address?"

"If I knew that, I wouldn't need you to find it."

"Of course. Anything else?"

"Yes. How are you doing? When was the last time you were paid?"

"When did you leave?"

"I've got money in my house. It's in the safe in my closet. I'll give you the combo."

"That's okay, I'm not starving. I can wait. What else do you need?"

"What's the name of that hair salon around here?"

"Kazamoo."

"Right. I need an appointment."

"They don't take walk-ins," she said.

"I'm not walking in. You're calling for an appointment."

"Same day is considered a walk-in. But I'll do what I can. So you're going to chop off your Samson-like locks?"

"All of it," I said.

"I liked it long. It was sexy."

"Yeah, well, you don't have to carry it."

"That sounds like something I've been saying to men for twenty years."

I grinned. "All right. Then I'll need a flight to Albuquerque. Then one to Amarillo."

"Albuquerque for the building?"

"Yes."

"And what's in Amarillo?"

"My friend Eddie, hopefully. And a waitress. I'll tell you about her later."

"Anything else?"

"That's all for now."

She sighed. "I'm glad you're okay. I was worried about you last night. Something told me that you were in trouble."

"You weren't wrong," I said. "It was close."

Her voice sounded anxious. "What does that mean?"

"Nothing," I said. "I'm here. I'm not going anywhere. Now just get me a haircut, please."

"Okay, boss," she said. I was about to hang up when she said, "By the way, what kind of property are you looking for in Albuquerque? A vacation home?"

"It's a warehouse."

"A warehouse? What are you going to put in it?"

"Broken men, mostly."

"Broken men?"

"Broken men and hope."

Chapter Thirty-Six

For far too long I've bought expensive clothing, hoping it would cover up a second-rate soul.

CHARLES JAMES'S DIARY

Amanda—after letting me know what a magician she was and that it usually took two months to get into the elite salon—informed me that she had booked me an appointment for that afternoon.

I opened the room's window as far as it would let me, then cleaned up the vomit from the floor, drank a cup of coffee, and took a long shower until my stomach started to settle.

The salon was only five blocks from the hotel. I didn't remember the last time I was there, just that I had been there several years before on one of my tours. It was the kind of place models, celebrities, and celebrity-wannabes frequented. One of the booths I walked by had a picture of the stylist standing next to Speaker of the House

Nancy Pelosi. My appointment was with a bald, handsome, bearded man named Sherman.

"How short do you want to go with your hair?" Sherman said.

"Quite short," I said. "I haven't cut it for two months."

"It's a little ragged," he said. "I'll take care of that. I'm thinking kind of a Hugh Jackman look."

I figured that was his segue into telling me that he did Hugh Jackman's hair. I was right. "Whenever Hugh's in town, he always drops by for a trim. The ladies here go lunatic. Why wouldn't they, you know? He's delectable. I just love that Aussie accent of his. So how do you want that luscious beard of yours groomed? We've got so much to work with. I can see sculpting it into an anchor, a Chiwetel Ejiofor look, or maybe a bit more full, an Andrew Lincoln. With your facial structure, a ducktail or a box would highlight your cheekbones."

"I just want it shaved off," I said.

"Tell me you're joking! That's like taking a chisel to the David."

I grinned. "Chisel away, Michelangelo. I want to see my face again."

Sherman looked like I had just asked for ketchup on my filet mignon. To his credit, he did as I asked. In the end, I don't know if I lost more hair from my head or my chin. There was a pile on the floor of both. Sherman finished his work by kneading hair cream back through my hair, then rubbing a face bracer on my cheeks.

"What do you think?" he asked, stepping away so I

could see myself in the mirror. "You look like a new man."

"More like a recycled one," I said.

Sherman laughed. "I'm going to use that," he said. "I don't know where, but I'm going to use that."

I walked away from the salon feeling like I'd lost five pounds off my face, or at least my head. Honestly, I didn't recognize myself. Of course, that meant that others might start recognizing me, but I wasn't worried about it anymore. It was only a matter of time before I outed myself. And besides, people had been reporting Elvis sightings for how many decades?

On my way back to the hotel I stopped to buy clothes at one of my favorite stops from my early success days—Stefano Ricci on Rodeo Drive. I had been there several times after I moved to Chicago. The store manager, Robbie, hadn't changed in eight years. He recognized me.

"Charles, you're back! It's so good to see you again. I thought I must have offended you."

"No. I live in Chicago now."

"Brutal town," he said. "And so cold. And all you've got is Lake Michigan, when you could have the Pacific and *moi*."

"How could I argue with that?" I said.

"You can't, my friend." He looked at me for a moment, then said, "It seems I read something about you awhile back. What was that? I remember it put me off."

"Probably that I was killed in a plane crash," I said.

"That's it. Whatever happened with that?"

I looked at a pair of jeans. "How much are these?" It was something I'd never asked in his store before.

"I don't know," he said, looking a little put off. "Let me look it up. . . . Okay, these jeans with Stefano's leather patch and hand-painted eagle are eighteen hundred dollars. And this beautiful tee, that would look lovely with it, is only nine hundred dollars."

Eighteen hundred dollars for a pair of jeans. All I could think of were the men in the shelter standing in line to get whatever pair of donated pants might fit them. I could practically clothe the whole shelter for that.

When I first started working the stage, McKay made me go out and buy new clothes. "You've got to look the part," he said. "You've got to look successful. Clothes don't make the man, but the wrong ones will destroy him." It took me 2,500 miles to realize that the *wrong* ones meant more than style.

To Robbie's dismay I left without buying anything. I looked online and found there was a Nordstrom's Rack nearby.

I found everything I needed at the store—shoes, jeans, shirts, the final bill coming in at less than five hundred dollars. I made a mental note to take the money I had just saved and buy clothes for the men in Albuquerque.

I got back to my room and took out my computer and, for the first time in a long time, checked my email. It was a little eerie how everything, except my spam, stopped after May 3.

I was looking for something from Eddie. Why didn't

he write? I still had the number for his wife, which I figured I could use as a last resort, though I doubted she would tell me where he was even if she knew. For all she knew I was an immigration officer.

I went to bed thinking about Gabriel, before pushing it away so I could sleep. One thing was for certain: I would walk all the way back to Chicago if I could do my life over again.

Chapter Thirty-Seven

The road to self-respect is uphill and is always walked alone.

CHARLES JAMES'S DIARY

I woke early, ready to get back to figuring out my life.

I took another long shower, still feeling out of place in the opulence of my surroundings—the marble-floored bathroom with gold-plated fixtures.

After getting dressed, I went through my pack, taking out everything I still needed, which wasn't much. I did come across the slip of paper on which Eddie had written his wife's phone number. I folded it into my pocket.

Then I took my pack (and all that was left in it) and went out for a walk. About six blocks from the hotel I came across a homeless man sitting on the ground with a sign.

Hungry. Please Help.

"Here," I said, shrugging off my pack. "There are all sorts of things in here. A pretty good tent and sleeping bag. Hope it helps." I started to walk away when the man shouted, "Hey!"

I turned back to him, and he said, "God bless, man."

I walked back to the hotel. Amanda had booked me on the 11:00 a.m. flight out of LA to Albuquerque.

I went to pack my things, then remembered that I'd given away my backpack. I put my computer in the hotel's laundry bag, kept my new clothes in the store sack, and then checked out of the hotel. The hotel's shuttle dropped me off half an hour later at LAX.

After making it through security I bought myself a vinyl carry-on bag, which I put my things in, then boarded my flight to New Mexico.

The flight from LAX to ABQ was only an hour and twenty-seven minutes. With the hour time change I landed at around two o'clock. I grabbed a taxi and headed directly downtown to the rescue mission.

The cab pulled up to the curb, and the driver looked back at me. "This really the place?"

"It really is," I said.

"I never dropped a fare off at a homeless shelter."

"First time for everything," I said. I paid him, then grabbed my bag and climbed out of the car.

The grounds around the warehouse were still crowded with homeless men.

I climbed the grate stairs. Like before, there were men standing at the top on the landing, but this time they turned away from me. It took me only a moment to understand. The last time I was there I looked like them. Now I looked like authority. I looked like "the man."

"How are you guys doing?" I asked.

"Fine, sir," one of the men said, avoiding eye contact.

I opened the door and walked into the small lobby area.

"Can I help you, sir?" a man asked.

Sir? The greeting threw me off. "Is Eric here?"

"He's in his office. Right around the corner."

"Thank you." I walked down the corridor. The room outside his office was crowded. Someone was playing the piano. Quite well, actually. I think he was playing Rachmaninoff.

I knocked on Eric's door. After a second time, his raspy voice came from the other side. He sounded annoyed. "It's not locked."

I slowly opened the door and stepped inside. Eric was sitting at his desk with his cowboy hat on. He looked at me for a moment, then sat up a little. He didn't recognize me. "Sorry," he said. "What can I do for you, sir?"

"Sir," I repeated. "What's with this 'sir' crap? It's me, Sundance."

Eric looked at me quizzically. "I'm sorry, have we met?"

I smiled. "Don't be sorry. It was just a few weeks ago." Then I added, "I had a beard back then."

"I don't recall."

"You invited me to the spend the night here."

Still nothing.

"One of your men had a heart attack out on the street. I think his name was Cliff—"

Suddenly Eric's eyes lit up. "Wait . . . you're not . . . Charles."

"Ah, you remembered."

"Well, you don't look the same." His eyes explored me. "What did you do, win the lottery?"

"I won it a while ago," I said. "And I finished my walk."

"To California," he said. "You were walking Route 66."

"That's right."

"So you finished your walk."

I nodded. "Yes, I did."

"Did you find what you wanted?"

"No. But maybe what I needed."

"That's the best explanation of life I've ever heard."

"Did Cliff make it?"

"Believe it or not, he did. I was sure he was gone. I guess the Big Guy wasn't ready to have him back yet. He's upstairs if you want to see him."

"That's okay," I said. "He wouldn't know me from Adam. I wouldn't mind seeing Justin again."

"Justin?"

"Big guy. Tattoo of a skull on his left arm. Works here."

"Oh, that Justin. He left for a few days. I don't know where he went, but he said he'll be back."

"Sorry I missed him," I said. "So, the last time we spoke you had some challenges. How are things going?"

His expression fell. "Not so good."

"Tell me about it."

"If you really want to know, I got a call from the landlord this morning. Some SOB put an offer on the place. He says the guy wants to take possession as soon as possible."

"Well, you can't put too much stock in that," I said. "You know how these deals fall through. Can't get financing, zoning problems, a hundred possibilities."

"Not this time. He said it's a cash deal, and the guy put down earnest money."

"Did he now," I said slowly. I looked at him for a moment, then said, "Actually, I knew that."

Eric looked at me quizzically. "How would you know that?"

"Because I'm the SOB who bought it."

"What?"

I reached into my bag and took out a couple of pieces of paper. "It's all right here. I've got a week to execute. There's a contract in there for you. You'll own the place outright, with a few stipulations. The main one being that it has to be used for its current function." I winked. "Just means you can't go selling it like a new piece of clothing with a sales tag."

He looked over the paperwork, then looked back up at me. "You have this kind of money?"

I nodded. "I do. Hebrews 13:2, 'for some have entertained angels unawares.'"

I noticed that his eyes were wet. "Why would you do this?"

"Why do you do what you do?"

"Because someone has to."

"Exactly," I said, and stood. "Well, congratulations on your new place."

"I still can't believe it." He stood and walked over to me. He hugged me. "God bless you, sir."

"He has. More than I deserve." I started to walk away, then turned back. "Do you want to get some dinner? I mean, somewhere other than your place?"

Eric smiled. "Yes. I think I would."

We had dinner at a small restaurant called Ben Michael's. The experience was basically like walking into some guy's house—or, to be more exact, Ben Michael's house. Ben, who is also the chef, waiter, and entertainment, doesn't have menus. He just tells you what he's making that day, which happened to be one of my favorites, chili relleno and enchiladas.

After dinner, Eric and I sat in the main room while Ben played Beatles songs on his piano. It was joyful. I don't know if it was the margaritas or the news that had liberated him most, but Eric looked like a new man.

I dropped Eric back off at the shelter while I spent the night at the Hotel Parq Central, which, I was told later, used to be an insane asylum and was haunted. I had considered staying in the shelter again, but, frankly, I needed the sleep.

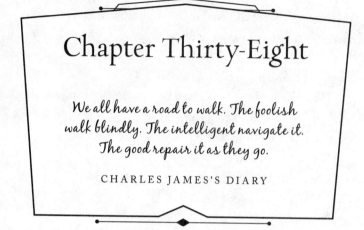

Chapter Thirty-Eight

We all have a road to walk. The foolish walk blindly. The intelligent navigate it. The good repair it as they go.

CHARLES JAMES'S DIARY

I called Amanda as I walked into my hotel room. "How'd it go?" she asked before I could speak.

"Well."

"Can you tell me what you're doing buying a homeless shelter in New Mexico?"

"When I was in Albuquerque I stayed in that homeless shelter. I found out that the man who ran the place was about to lose his building. I decided to buy it for him."

She was silent for a moment, then said, "That's beautiful."

"It's the right thing to do," I replied. "Now, on to the next project. I need you to book me the next flight to Amarillo."

"Just a minute; let me check the flights. There's nothing direct from ABQ to Amarillo. There's an early bird on American at 6:39, arriving at noon, or an eight o'clock on United—no, scratch that. It's seven hours with two layovers. There's an 11:12, arriving at 3:49."

"I'll take it. I'll need a hotel. You can book me in the same Marriott we stayed in last time. And I'll need a car. A nice one this time. I'm trying to make a point."

"Nice as in a McLaren?"

"No. Down a few grades. Try a Mercedes."

"Mercedes it is. Convertible?"

"Sure. It will feel good to have wind in my hair."

"At least what's left of it," she said. "I'll text you the confirmation."

I arrived in Amarillo too late to make Plainview, so I drove straight to the hotel, went out for an early dinner, and then came back and watched a documentary on Prohibition. I didn't know that it was Prohibition that gave us a federal income tax and organized crime. Bad deal all around. I fell asleep during an episode on Al Capone.

I woke the next morning at seven, showered, and drove out. I stopped for a coffee at the 7-Eleven where I'd first met Eddie and boarded the truck for Plainview, Texas. I was excited at the thought of seeing Eddie again, and the seventy-five-mile drive seemed interminable. The last time I took this trip I was hairy, broke, and riding in the back of an open pickup truck. That's when Eddie told me that the Jimmy Dean sausage guy was from Plainview. I smiled at the memory.

I got a little lost in Plainview, since I'd never driven it, but eventually made it to the cotton fields. The migrant workers were in the fields, well into their workday. The weeds we had assaulted were gone, and they were now picking cotton bolls. Curtis, the foreman I'd nicknamed Simon Legree, was standing next to his truck. I pulled up alongside him in my Mercedes.

"How goes it, Curtis?" I asked.

He looked at me quizzically. "Fine. Who are you?"

"You don't recognize me?"

"Can't say I do."

"When I worked for you, you called me Frank. As in Frank Lloyd Wright. It was your little joke."

He just looked at me. "When you worked for me?"

"You had me picking pigweed," I said.

He still couldn't place me. "What do you want?"

"I'm looking for someone. One of the workers who was here with me. His name was Eddie."

"He's not here."

"How do you know?"

"Because I don't see him."

"Do you have any contact information for him?"

"I've got work to do," he said, starting to turn away.

"Hold on, partner," I said to him. "Let me lay this out for you. I know you're wondering why one of your workers is driving a car you couldn't afford. I'll tell you. I was working here undercover. I'm a bestselling author, and I wanted to document how American farmers treat migrant workers. I couldn't have chosen a better place. You gave me some interesting things to write about."

Curtis looked rattled. "You defame me, I'll sue," he said.

I laughed. "You could try," I said. "You'd have to prove malice, which you can't—or that what I was writing was willfully false, which you can't either, thereby indicting yourself. Besides, you'll be too busy running from the social-justice lynch mobs and your own employers, who would happily throw you under the thresher to save their own hides. And we both know that you haven't got the money to prosecute a case like this. It would cost you a fortune."

"It will cost you a fortune, too."

"It won't cost me a dime. Because after you lose, you'll have my legal fees, too. Besides, my lawyers are on retainer."

Curtis looked defeated. "What do you want?"

"I'm looking for Eddie."

"I told you, I don't know where he is."

"You're going to have to try harder than that," I said. "You don't have any records?"

"You saw how we run things. We pay in cash. He's an illegal. You think we're going to keep records?"

"Mind if I look around?"

"Help yourself," he said. "Won't do you any good."

"We'll see," I said.

I got back in my car and drove to where the workers were. I walked more than a mile up and down the rows but didn't recognize anyone. Hardly anyone would even look at me, and when I tried to speak to them, they either didn't speak English or didn't know who Eddie was.

I got into my car and drove to the farm's office, where Curtis had fled.

"Find your man?" he asked as I walked inside.

"No," I said.

"I told you it wouldn't do you any good. It's like finding a fish in the ocean. They don't tell us where they're going. They just blow in and blow out. When they finish here, they go off somewhere else. Your friend could be picking apples in Michigan, spuds in Idaho, or blueberries in California."

"All right," I said. I grabbed a piece of paper and wrote my name and phone number on it. "If you ever see him, call me. I'll pay you a five-hundred-dollar reward."

He looked at the paper, then back up at me. "What about your book? Are you still going to write about me?"

"I'm thinking about it," I said. "You find him, I won't." I got into my car and drove away.

Chapter Thirty-Nine

This must be how Saint Nicholas feels.

CHARLES JAMES'S DIARY

For lunch I had fried green tomatoes and a slightly burnt chicken-fried steak with green beans and cream gravy at the Cotton Patch Café in Plainview (I think the cook put extra gravy on the steak to camouflage the burnt parts), then drove back to Amarillo, arriving at the hotel at around three in the afternoon.

I picked up a FedEx package Amanda had sent me and then went back out, walking around downtown Amarillo just to stretch my legs. I stopped at the Burrowing Owl bookstore for a book on learning Italian.

A little after five o'clock I headed off to my next stop, forty-five miles away in Groom, Texas.

About two-thirds of the way to Groom I passed the small town of Conway. It's the town where I had stopped at a bank to get money, only to realize that all my account numbers were in my smartphone. There I was, stranded without any ID, broke, unshaven, unbathed, basically looking as homeless as I was, telling the bank clerk that I was a multimillionaire with an offshore account in the Cayman Islands. I'm surprised she didn't call the police or the nearest mental care professional. I was tempted to stop and visit the clerk.

The drive from Amarillo looked different than I remembered. The most peculiar thing was that I had somehow missed the Groom Cross, one of the largest Christian crosses in the world. The monument, just a little southwest of Groom, is nineteen stories tall and can be seen for more than twenty miles. Yet in my state of mind, or circumstance, I somehow didn't see it. I guess I wasn't looking for it. Maybe there's a message there.

The Grill-Welcome Home diner was only slightly busier than it had been during my last visit—a half-dozen people scattered throughout the small café. At first I didn't see my waitress, Brenda; only another woman who walked up to seat me. "Just one?" she asked, lifting a menu from the counter.

"Just me," I said. "Is Brenda here today?"

"Yes."

"I'd like to sit in her station," I said. "We're friends."

She nodded. "You got it."

Coincidentally, she led me to the same table where I had sat when I had come before, penniless and hungry.

A few minutes later, Brenda walked out of the back. She looked the same as before, still pretty, still weary looking. She was carrying a glass of ice water. The other waitress must have told her that I had said we were friends, because she looked at me with a slightly concerned expression, and I guessed that she was trying to figure out who I was without offending me. I didn't assume she would recognize me. She set the water glass down on the table.

"Hi. How are you?" she said.

"Good," I said. "And you?"

"Good. It's good to see you again," she said weakly.

"It's good to be seen again," I said. I just looked at her for a moment, then smiled. "You have no idea who I am, do you?"

She shook her head. "Not a clue."

I laughed. "Really? You don't remember me? I came through here a couple of months ago."

"I'm sorry. A lot of people come through here."

"I'm just kidding. I didn't expect you to recognize me. I looked a lot different back then. I had a beard and long hair, and I was carrying a pack. I had just been robbed by a motorcycle gang."

I could see the light of recognition come to her eyes. "Oh, wait. You're that Route 66 guy . . . you were on a pilgrimage."

"Right; you called me Pilgrim." I looked into her eyes. "And you gave me back the hundred dollars they'd stolen from me."

"I remember now. You clean up well."

"So I've been told." I reclined against the vinyl seat and smiled. "How's your day, Brenda?"

She sighed. "Well, Pilgrim, you know, just like yesterday. And the day before. And the day before that. No doubt tomorrow will be the same."

"No, tomorrow won't ever be the same again."

She grinned. "No?"

"Not if you don't want it to be. First, I told you that I would pay you back, remember?" I took out a crisp hundred-dollar bill and handed it to her. "There you go."

"You don't need to . . ."

"Come on," I said. "We both know you need it."

She took the bill. "Thank you."

"You're welcome."

"You came all the way back here to give me a hundred dollars?"

"No. There's more. Do you remember that I asked you something like, what if I were a multimillionaire who could make your dreams come true? And you said something like, 'I'd say you're . . .'"

"'. . . a bigger dreamer than I am,'" she finished. "I remember that."

"Well, I am a big dreamer. In fact, I've spent my life selling dreams, you might say. But I'm also a multimillionaire. And you helped me when I needed help. So now I'm going to make your dreams come true." I handed her a business card.

TOLMAN TRAVEL AND ADVENTURES

Cameron Tolman

President

Corporate • Personal • Nuptial

She scanned the card, then looked back up at me quizzically. "What's this?"

"Cameron's a friend of mine. He owns one of the top travel agencies in Chicago. My firm has used his agency for years. Unless you've changed your mind, you said you wanted to go to Venice and find yourself a handsome Italian, right?"

She laughed. "I couldn't possibly afford—"

"I know," I interrupted. "That's why I've arranged for Cameron to book a first-class flight for you to Venice, and he's already found you an apartment in Rossini, near Piazza San Marco. That's in Venice, if you don't know. He's just waiting for my word to sign the lease. I think a year should be sufficient for you to find Mr. *Fantastico.* Knowing the men in Italy, that might be eleven months too long."

Brenda just stared at me. "I don't understand."

"Of course you do," I said. "You, of all people, understand helping someone in need." I reached into my pocket. "Oh, and you'll need this." I handed her an envelope.

She pried off the top of the envelope. It was filled with newly printed hundred-dollar bills.

"There are fifty Benjamins in there," I said. "I suspected that you'd need a little cash to get out of Dodge."

She just looked at the envelope, then handed it back to me. "This is so generous, but I can't let you do this."

"You *can't*? Of course you can. The only question is *will* you?"

Her eyes started to moisten. "I . . . I only have a few hundred dollars in savings," she said. "What if I can't get a job in Italy?"

"I don't want you to get a job," I said. "Neither does the Italian government. They want Americans to bring them jobs, not take them." I handed her the plastic card Amanda had overnighted me. "This is a debit card in both of our names. In addition to covering your rent, I'll deposit three thousand dollars into it each month. That's more than enough to live on. Don't use more than that, because you'll run out." I looked her in the eyes. "Oh, I brought this, too." I handed her a book: *Italian for Dummies*.

"Not that it will hinder the men any, but you'll want to brush up on your Italian. There's a good Italian language school in Rossini. I had my assistant check on it. Their next course starts in two weeks. They still have room if you'd like to enroll. Now, the only question is, do you have the courage to chase your dream?"

"What if I fail?"

I smiled. "What if you don't? Besides, the worst thing that can happen to you is that you'll have the experience of a lifetime."

Brenda took a napkin from a nearby table and wiped her eyes. "Why are you doing this? Why are you helping me like this?"

"I asked you that very thing," I said softly. "And I loved your answer. Do you remember what you said?"

She shook her head.

"You said, 'Because you needed help.'"

She wiped her eyes again. "You're a good man."

"Now you're getting carried away. I just want to set a few things right."

She wiped her eyes, then leaned into my chest and cried. I put my arms around her.

"God bless you," she said.

I kissed the top of her head and pulled her in tight. "I think He just did."

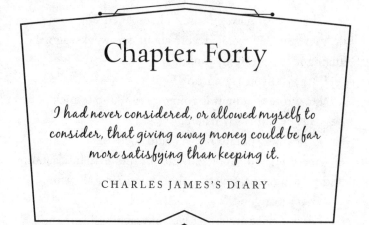

Chapter Forty

I had never considered, or allowed myself to consider, that giving away money could be far more satisfying than keeping it.

CHARLES JAMES'S DIARY

I really wanted to wait around to see Brenda quit her job, but her boss wasn't there and she said she couldn't just leave the other waitress in the lurch, which I respected. I wrote down my phone number for her, and then, after she hugged me again, I drove back to Amarillo. I called Amanda on the way.

"How did it go?" she asked.

"It was . . . fun," I said.

"Fun? I haven't heard you say that in a long time."

"Don't quote me, but there might actually be something to that saying, 'It's better to give than to receive.'"

"You think?"

"I'll let you know. I'm still processing this."

"So, I have good news. Well, it's sort of good news. I found Eddie."

"That's *great* news," I said. "He emailed?"

"Actually he emailed you about six weeks ago. His email got caught in my junk file."

"Why did you say 'sort of'?"

"He wrote that he was going up to Idaho to pick potatoes. But he didn't say where."

"How many potato farms could there be?"

"According to Google, there are more than six hundred potato farms, covering more than 309,000 acres."

"That's not good."

"Do you have any other way of reaching him?"

"His wife, maybe. But getting her to talk will be tricky."

"Why is that?"

"A strange American calls looking for her husband, an undocumented immigrant? She's going to assume I'm either from immigration or the police."

"Why don't you have someone else call?"

"Like who?"

"Someone Mexican. You're in Texas; I'm sure you can find someone Hispanic."

"You're brilliant," I said.

"That's why I make the big bucks," she said.

When I got back to the hotel, I found the phone number that Eddie had written down, then I went down to the lobby. One of the clerks at the hotel was Mexican.

"Excuse me," I said, looking at his name tag. "Jesus?"

"Yes, sir. How may I help you?"

"Do you speak Spanish?"

"*Sí.* I am Mexican."

"I didn't want to assume," I said. "I'm Mexican, too.

My last name is Gonzales and I speak Spanish, but not well. I need help translating. I'll pay you." I held out a hundred-dollar bill.

"There's no need to pay me, sir," he said. "I'd be happy to help."

"Thank you," I said. "This is my dilemma." I explained the situation, including who I was and the time I'd spent in Plainview. After about ten minutes I handed him the phone number. "That's the number he gave me for his wife. What do you think?"

"I will try," he said. "But we should go back to the office for privacy." He turned to his coworker, a young woman with straight, strawberry-blond hair and thick tortoise-shell glasses. "Miss Lindsey, I need to help this guest. I will be right back."

"I'm good," she said.

"Come with me," Jesus said. "Please walk around the side."

I walked past the counter to a half door that led back to an office with two small cubicles. He sat down at a desk and gestured to a chair in the cubicle next to him. "Please, have a seat."

"Thank you," I said.

He dialed the number. A moment later he said, "Hello, I am calling for Senorita Felicia de la Cruz." I could hear someone shouting. "I am very sorry, I did not realize that it was so late. I am calling from Texas. Yes, ma'am, it is very important. Thank you." He looked up at me. "This number is in Florida. It is past eleven o'clock. She was very angry."

"Sorry," I said.

"No problem."

In my eagerness to find Eddie I had forgotten the time difference. It was several minutes before anyone answered. "*Hola, señorita. Perdoneme por la llamada tarde. Estoy llamando en Texas . . . Soy el senor Gomez. Soy un amigo de tu esposo Eddie . . . No, el esta bien.*"

Jesus spoke fast enough that I lost track of much of what was said, but I got the gist of it. At first Felicia was clearly suspicious, but he eventually broke through. About five minutes into the conversation he grabbed a pen and began writing something down.

"*Muchas gracias, señorita.*" He hung up the phone, then looked up at me. "He is in Idaho, where he is picking potatoes."

"Did she say where in Idaho?"

"This place." He handed me the paper.

R K Spuds
Pocatello, Idaho

I knew Pocatello. It was less than two hours north of where I grew up in northern Utah. I looked up and smiled. "Thank you."

"I am happy to help. Good luck finding your friend."

Chapter Forty-One

There's another visit I need to make. I don't suppose that this reception will be as welcoming as the others.

CHARLES JAMES'S DIARY

I called Amanda when I got back to my room. "I found Eddie. He's working at a farm in Pocatello."

"I thought he was in Idaho."

"Pocatello *is* in Idaho."

"Sorry. My bad."

"I need a flight and a car."

"Does Pocatello have an airport?"

"Yes. A small one."

"Let me look it up." A moment later she said, "It's not good. All the flights have at least two layovers, Denver and Salt Lake. The shortest flight is more than eight hours. You could fly to London in that time."

"How about a direct flight to Salt Lake?"

"Let's see. No. Everything goes through Denver. But Denver to Salt Lake isn't bad."

"Let's do that. It's only a two-hour drive to Pocatello from Salt Lake. I'll need a car."

"Got it. I'll call you back."

I hung up, then lay back on the bed. My phone rang fifteen minutes later.

"Your flight to Salt Lake leaves tomorrow morning at eight ten a.m. and arrives in Salt Lake at eleven-oh-five."

"Thank you."

"You're welcome. When will you be coming back to Chicago?"

"I don't know. I've got at least one more visit on the way."

"With who?"

"I'll let you know when I find out."

Chapter Forty-Two

I've changed. Why, then, did I expect everything and everyone else to stay the same?

CHARLES JAMES'S DIARY

My flight landed on time in Salt Lake. I picked up an economy rental car. The extra visit I'd mentioned to Amanda was one I'd thought over for a very long time. It was one I never thought I'd make. The drive from Salt Lake to Pocatello would take me up I-15 through my hometown of Ogden. I had decided to stop there to see my father, or whatever family of mine still occupied the house.

The last time I'd been home was more than a decade earlier, just before I married Monica. I'd come through town on a seminar and taken the opportunity to drive up to see my family for the first time in years. Only my father was there. The visit hadn't gone well. My father's foot had just been amputated from complications of diabetes. After all these years, there was a better than even chance that he wasn't alive. I would find out soon enough.

The drive from Salt Lake to Ogden took less than an hour. As I drove east toward the Wasatch mountain range, Ben Lomond Peak rose nearly ten thousand feet to the north of me. It was a familiar site from my childhood, and I had climbed the mountain alone as a teenager. It wasn't easy, but it was something I'd set my mind on. Besides, few things were easy in my youth.

Interesting fact—you might be more familiar with that mountain peak than you know. William Hodkinson, the founder of Paramount Pictures, spent much of his youth in Ogden, Utah. It's also where he opened his first movie theater. It's believed that Ben Lomond Peak was the inspiration for the iconic Paramount Pictures logo, which Hodkinson sketched on a napkin based on memories of his youth in Ogden.

The last time I'd gone home I'd purposely driven a Cadillac. It was important for me back then to show my father that I had made something of my life—not for the purpose of filling him with pride for his son's success. I had no such delusion. I'd driven the car to rub his face in it—to show him that I'd succeeded where he'd failed. Or, at least, that I had succeeded in spite of him.

This time I had no such desire. Nor such a car, for that matter. I was driving a Chevy Malibu. I also had little expectation that he would be happy to see me. His last words still rang in my memory: "You left, you stay gone. You're not welcome here, boy."

I almost missed the turnoff to my home. The city had changed. Growing up, our neighborhood had been fairly isolated. Now there was a Walmart less than a quarter mile from the house, allied with the usual fast-food chains—an Olive Garden, a Subway, a Burger King, and a Chick-fil-A. When I had lived there we only had Woody's Drive Inn—a one-of-a-kind drive-through that served chocolate sodas and malts as well as the usual fried fare indigenous to such homegrown eateries.

I drove slowly down the old lane. Even that had changed. Before, most of it had been dirt road with an irrigation ditch running alongside it. It was now all asphalt with smooth cement curbs and sidewalks, an occasional grate revealing where the waterway still existed.

The vacant lots where my brother, Mike, and I had once played had sprouted homes with manicured landscaping. Behind the lane was a new subdivision of town homes.

Then I saw the house. While the world moved on around it, the old house remained like an island in time. But even it had changed some. Most of the trees I remembered had been cleared away, and there was a new garage built onto the side of the house.

My father's old truck wasn't there. I don't know why that surprised me, except that, in my memory, it was just as much a fixture of the house as the front porch. Where the truck was usually parked, there was now a pearl-white Toyota Avalon. It occurred to me that the house had likely been sold.

I parked my car in front of the home and walked up the concrete pathway to the front door, which had been painted a pleasant dusty blue and hung with a wreath.

I went to knock but noticed that the doorbell—which hadn't worked for as long as I remembered—had been replaced. I rang it. A minute later a woman with long, dark hair and beautiful almond-shaped eyes opened the door.

"May I help you?"

"I'm sorry, I was looking for someone who used to live here. My father."

"Are you sure you have the right address?"

"I'm sure of that. I used to live here."

She looked at me for a moment then said, "No one has ever lived here but my husband's family."

"Your husband," I said. The light went on. "Are you Michael's wife?"

She slowly nodded. "You know Michael?"

"I'm Michael's brother, Charles."

She looked at me quizzically. "My husband's brother was killed in a plane crash."

"I know," I said. "That's what everyone thinks. Is Michael here?"

She looked anxious. I could tell that she was still processing my appearance. "He should be back in a few minutes."

"How long have you and Michael been married?"

"Eight years," she said. "Almost nine."

"It's been that long," I said, shaking my head.

"You do look like Mike," she said. After a moment she added, "Would you like to come in?"

"Thank you." I stepped inside, and she shut the door behind me. The house had been drastically remodeled. The last time I'd been there the room had been dark and smelled of mold. Now it was light and smelled of lavender and honey.

"You've redone the house."

"It was needed."

"It was pretty disgusting," I said.

She slightly nodded. "There was mold. We had to strip everything down to the drywall." She gestured to the sofa. "Please, have a seat."

"Thank you." I walked over and sat down.

"May I get you something to drink? A soda? I've got limeade."

"A limeade would be great."

Limeade. Mike always loved lime rickeys from Woody's. She walked out of the room, returning just a moment later with a tall glass. "Here you go."

"Thank you."

She sat down in a chair across from me.

I took a sip of my drink, then asked, "What's your name?"

"It's Stacy."

"It's nice to meet you, Stacy."

She just looked at me for a moment, then asked, "Why does everyone think you're dead?"

"Well, it's a peculiar situation. Six months ago I had just boarded a flight in Chicago when I realized that I'd left my laptop at a store in the terminal, so I left the plane. By the time I got back they'd closed the Jetway and the flight attendant had left. They had me checked in, so when the flight crashed, the airline's records showed that I was still on it." I shrugged. "Everyone thinks I'm dead."

"Why didn't you tell them you weren't?"

"That's complicated."

"Michael . . ." she hesitated. "It was hard on him. It was really hard on your mother."

"Where is my mother?"

"She lives in an assisted living center in Bountiful."

Bountiful is a bedroom community just north of Salt Lake.

"I don't even know if my father is still alive."

"He lives in the same place."

"With my mother?"

"They got back together."

Her news surprised me on both counts. "That's . . . unexpected."

She nodded slightly.

"I'm surprised he's still alive. The last time I saw him, he had just had his foot amputated."

"He's not doing well. The diabetes is slowly killing him. He's blind now." She suddenly breathed out heavily. "I don't know how Mike is going to handle seeing you. His feelings for you are, like you said, complicated." She looked upset. "You dying doesn't make things any less complicated."

"I wouldn't think so." A moment later I added, "I'm sorry."

We were both quiet. Then we heard a vehicle pull up along the side of the house. "That's Mike."

A moment later the back door opened. Then a deep voice boomed, "Hey, Stace, is someone here?"

"We're in here," she said.

He walked into the room. "Who's . . ." He froze when he saw me.

So did time. It seemed a long while before anyone spoke. Finally I said, "Hey, Mike."

Mike looked pale and said nothing. After a moment I stood. "The prodigal brother returns. Are you going to welcome me?"

Mike looked at his wife, then back at me. "You're supposed to be dead."

"Rumors of my death were exaggerated."

He didn't respond. After a moment he said, "Why aren't you dead?"

Stacy's eyes darted back and forth between us.

"I've been asking myself that same thing," I said.

"He wasn't really on the plane," Stacy explained.

Suddenly Mike's anger surfaced. "You left me. You left me here alone."

"I didn't leave you. I left Dad."

"You left me, too. I needed you."

"I'm sorry, Mike. But I was a teenager. Dad didn't hate you like he did me. He almost killed me. If I'd stayed, he might have."

Mike just stood there, emotionally wavering, as if unsure which way he would fall. I walked over to him. "I'm sorry I left you. I had to go."

His eyes filled with tears. "I never thought I'd see you again."

"I know," I said. "I'm so sorry. I tried to find you, but I couldn't."

He suddenly broke down. I put my arms around him, resting my head against his. "I never stopped thinking of you."

When he could speak he said, "I never stopped thinking of you, too."

Chapter Forty-Three

What a peculiar alchemist is time—
transforming painful experiences into comedy.

CHARLES JAMES'S DIARY

I spent the entire evening with them. We ended up going to dinner at a new sushi restaurant (new to me) and, after several glasses of hot sake, did our best to fill in for each other the main happenings from the decades we'd been apart. Mike kept telling me how much he bragged to others about my success, as a big-time author and presenter, but I was just as proud of the man he'd become and all he'd accomplished. He had a good job as an information systems analyst for Lockheed Martin at Hill Air Force Base, just twenty minutes south of Ogden. I was happy to see him doing so well. Halfway through dinner I asked, "Are there any plans for children?"

Mike and Stacy glanced at each other, then Michael took her hand. "We've been going through infertility for the last five years," Stacy said. "It hasn't worked. Now we're trying to adopt."

"It's been a rough road," Mike said. "How about you? Any children?"

"I have a son," I said. "But . . ." I paused. "We got divorced. My wife and child live in California."

"I'm sorry," Mike said.

"Me, too," I said.

We ate a little more. Then I said, "Stacy said that Mom and Dad are back together."

Mike nodded. "They're in the care center together. We tried to take care of them here, but with my work schedule, it pretty much just all fell on Stacy. It was too much. Dad's diabetes is taking him apart. First it took his feet, then his eyes. He's been blind for four years now. Now he's lost two of his fingers. I don't think he's going to last much longer."

I felt sympathy for him.

"How is Mom's health?"

"Her back has gotten worse. And now she has Parkinson's."

I shook my head. "I remember when she hurt her back," I said. "That's how she lost her nursing job."

"I remember," Mike said. "That's when she started selling Avon."

"*We*," I said. "I ended up doing most of the selling."

"I almost forgot," Mike said. He turned to Stacy. "Charles was the most successful teenage boy to ever sell Avon."

"I was the *only* teenage boy to ever sell Avon. Man, I got teased about it."

"Made you strong," Mike said.

"That it did." I breathed out. "How advanced is Mom's Parkinson's?"

"She has tremors, but she doesn't complain."

"She never does."

"Except when she heard that you died. That was rough on her. She took to bed for a month."

"I'm sorry."

"Are you going to go see them?"

"I want to. Do you think I should?"

"Definitely."

"The last time I saw Dad he said he never wanted to see me again."

"I know."

"He told you?"

Mike nodded. "He's changed."

"In what way?"

"He regrets how he treated us."

I was quiet a moment, then said, "I have regrets, too."

"Everyone has regrets," Mike said seriously. He looked at his wife. "Even Stacy."

"I don't have regrets," Stacy said.

He looked back at me. "She should. She married me."

Stacy laughed and hit him. "Stop it."

After dinner we drove back to the house. Stacy made us coffee and the three of us just sat in the front room talking.

"I shouldn't keep you up so late," I said.

"I haven't seen my brother in sixteen years; I can lose a little sleep," Mike said. "Speaking of which, remember when you used to have to get up at four in the morning to go Dumpster diving?"

"You think I could forget that?"

"You used to do what?" Stacy asked.

"My dad used to take Charles out every Saturday morning and throw him in the Dumpster to see what he could find."

Stacy looked shocked. "That's horrible."

"It was like fishing," I said. "You never knew what you'd find."

"You'd come back stinking like trash."

I laughed, too. "Came with the territory."

"I can't believe you two are laughing about this," Stacy said.

"He laughs so he doesn't cry," Mike said.

"Looking back on it, it really is kind of funny. Except that time I found a corpse in one."

"A dead one?" Stacy said.

"All corpses are dead," Mike said. "Otherwise, they're called people."

Stacy ignored him. "Did you call the police?"

"I was, like, eight," I said. "And no, my father was sure he'd get blamed for it."

"Just horrific," Stacy said. "I don't know how you two survived childhood."

"That which doesn't kill you only makes you stronger," Mike said. "Except bears. Bears will kill you."

"Actually, that experience paid off," I said. "I must have shared that story a thousand times from the stage. It brought in millions of dollars."

"Ah," Mike sighed. "I'm in the wrong business."

The room suddenly fell into silence.

"Where are you staying, Charles?" Stacy asked.

"I'm not sure. I was headed up to Pocatello. I was going to find a hotel there."

"What's in Pocatello?" Mike asked.

"Someone I need to help."

"Why don't you stay here for the night?" Stacy said.

"Of course he will," Mike said. "He's a Gonzales. He doesn't need a bidet."

I laughed. "Do you have room?"

"We have a guest room," Mike said. "Actually, it's our old bedroom. If that's not too traumatic."

The idea of sleeping in my childhood bedroom filled me with mixed emotions. But maybe I could lay some of the demons to rest. "Sounds good to me."

"Good," Stacy said. "I need to put some fresh sheets on. I'll let you boys finish catching up." She walked over and kissed Mike, then came over and hugged me. "Thank you for coming, Charles. It means more than you know." She left the room.

After she was gone I said, "You've married a beautiful woman. Inside and out."

"You got that right," he said.

"Where did you meet?"

"Weber State. She was a computer science major." He looked at me. "If you don't mind me asking, what happened to your marriage?"

I looked down for a moment, then, knitting my fingers, looked into his eyes. "I cheated on her."

I think my honesty surprised him. "Oh."

"I've regretted it every day since."

"I'm sorry." He looked at me. "You know, your death made national news."

"It means nothing," I said.

"It means something," he said. "So where have you been since the crash? Hiding from the paparazzi?"

"I walked Route 66."

He looked at me. "The whole way?"

"Every inch."

"How far is that?"

"Almost twenty-five hundred miles."

"That's unbelievable," he said. "So when are you going to resurface? I mean, to the public."

"I don't know."

"You know it will be big news when you do. They'll have you on all the morning shows."

"All the more reason not to resurface," I said. "But it's inevitable, I suppose. Or else the courts will start distributing my assets."

"You'd better start thinking about that." He stifled a yawn.

"It's getting late. Do you have work in the morning?"

"Oh yeah."

"What time do you start?"

"Zero-freaking six hundred."

"Six a.m. Now I feel guilty."

"Don't," he said. His voice lowered. "You know, part of me expects to wake in the morning and find out that this was all a dream. I've missed you, man. You know, you were always my hero. Even after you left."

"You can do better in the hero department," I said.

"I'm not so sure of that." He was suddenly quiet. "I never told you something. That night that Dad almost beat you to death. I knew that he was beating you because he caught you with my *Playboy.* I was always ashamed about that. I should have done something. Instead I just cowered in my bed."

"There's nothing you could have done. You were just a boy."

"I doesn't matter. I should have tried something."

"It does matter," I said curtly. "You were a boy. Children always think they can control things they can't. There's nothing you could have done. Nothing. And I couldn't let him hurt you. If he hurt you, that would have been worse."

He just shook his head. "I never stopped feeling ashamed for that. When I heard that you had died, I knelt down and told you how sorry I was. I figured that maybe you would be able to hear me. At least you can now."

"You were just a boy," I said again. "You shouldn't feel shame for something you did as a boy." A few minutes later I said, "I really need to let you sleep."

"Do you have a bag?"

"It's in the car. I'll get it." I went out and grabbed my suitcase, then brought it back in. Mike was standing at the end of the hallway near our old room. "Here you go," he said. "If you need anything, you know where to find it. The bathroom's in the same place."

"Thank you." We embraced. Mike just held on to me. "Thank you for not dying," he said. I knew he was talking about the plane crash, but he had no idea how much that meant to me after almost taking my own life.

I put my bag down in the bedroom, then went into the bathroom to brush my teeth. Like the rest of the house, the bathroom had been redone, from the new stone tile floor to the porcelain sink and pewter fixtures. The space was smaller than I remembered. I have found that we remember things from our childhood as being bigger than they really were. Maybe that's true of our childhood experiences as well. Still, the intensity of that night in the bathroom would be hard to exaggerate. My father had beaten me unconscious. I had lain on the floor in my own blood and urine and climbed into the tub to clean myself off. I had lost God that day. I don't think I'd made it bigger than it really was.

But that day, like my youth, was past, and the room was bright and clean and innocent, as if it held no memories.

I finished brushing my teeth, then returned to the guest room.

That space was different, too. There had once been two small beds. I remembered hiding under my bed from my drunken father. Now there was only one queen-sized bed next to a side table with a robin's-egg blue vase-shaped lamp with an ivory shade and a hand-thrown pottery bowl filled with potpourri. I lay back in the bed and closed my eyes to it all.

I wondered if this was how a soldier felt returning to a battlefield decades after the war had ended.

Chapter Forty-Four

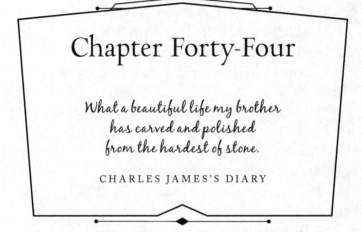

What a beautiful life my brother
has carved and polished
from the hardest of stone.

CHARLES JAMES'S DIARY

I was a little surprised that I didn't have either dreams or nightmares that night. I woke the next morning to the smell of coffee and bacon.

I put on my gym shorts and a T-shirt and walked out to the kitchen. Stacy was standing next to the stove in her robe, holding a spatula. She looked happy to see me. "Good morning."

"Morning," I replied.

"How did you sleep?"

"I slept well, thank you. Is Mike gone?"

"Yes." She handed me a cup of coffee. "There's sugar and cream on the table." She turned back to the stove. "He leaves early. Especially this morning. They called at four with some problem he had to go in for."

"He got, like, four hours' sleep," I said.

"Less." She smiled. "It's his own fault. He wanted to be with you. Would you like hotcakes?"

"I would love hotcakes," I said. I sat down at the table.

"He wanted me to tell you to call him when you got up."

"Thank you."

"Are you staying with us another day?"

"No. I'm headed up to Pocatello. But I'll stop by on the way back."

She brought over a small glass of grapefruit juice, then a plate with two pancakes, three strips of bacon, and a pitcher of syrup. "I need to get ready. Help yourself to whatever you like. There's more coffee in the pot."

She walked out of the kitchen. I ate my breakfast, went back to the bedroom and put on my shoes, then went out for a walk. It was a warm August morning, dry but pleasant. The air was thinner than I was used to.

It felt nice to be out and walking, which I found myself doing more for the sake of exploration than for exercise. I couldn't believe how much had changed in the old neighborhood. Every home I remembered was gone, bulldozed for new construction.

When I got back to the house, Stacy was standing near the door dressed in a bright sundress and looking through her purse. She looked up at me and smiled. "How was your walk?"

"Refreshing," I said.

"I'll be out for a couple of hours," she said. "Will you still be here when I get back?"

"No. I'm going to shower, then go."

"All right." She came over and hugged me again. "Welcome home, Charles. We're so glad you're back. This family needs you more than you'll ever know."

Chapter Forty-Five

I have found what I was looking for. And I suppose that doesn't just mean Eddie.

CHARLES JAMES'S DIARY

I took a shower and dressed. This time I didn't have a second thought about the bathroom. I guess I'd forgiven it. I packed my few things, then carried them out to my car. I had thought all night about seeing my parents, but I wasn't sure if it would be this trip or a future one. The reunion with Mike had been more than I could have hoped for. I guess I didn't want to push my luck.

I called Amanda on my drive back to I-15.

"Where are you?" she asked like she always did.

"I should just wear a GPS monitor," I said.

"Don't think I haven't thought about it. Did you find Eddie?"

"I found my brother," I said. "I spent the night at his house."

"That's good, isn't it?"

"Yeah. It's good," I said. "Now I'm headed up to Pocatello to find Eddie. Tell me, what's Marissa's situation with the boys?"

"I don't understand the question."

"Does she have a nanny?"

"Funny you should ask that. Up until now, she hasn't. McKay was very much against it. But now that she's alone, she needs the help. When I called her yesterday she asked if I had any experience finding a nanny."

"Live-in or part-time?"

"She was thinking live-in. Their home has a small guesthouse in back. A casita."

"That's too perfect," I said. "Tell her I've got a nanny for her. As well as someone to maintain her cars, yard, and home."

"You mean Felicia and Eddie?"

"Exactly."

"You're brilliant," she said.

"Call her, then call me back."

Amanda called back before I made it to the Idaho border. "Marissa was almost in tears," she said. "She said it would be perfect. There was just one thing. She was worried about the cost. Her financial advisor told her she can only afford twenty-five hundred a month, plus the casita."

"That will be enough," I said. "And check the flights out tomorrow from Salt Lake to Miami."

The drive from Ogden to Pocatello was a fairly boring one, and I found myself laying out how it would be walked, mentally making camp every twenty miles. I stayed on I-15 north for two and a half hours, then took the 86 west turnoff toward Bannock and the potato farm.

R&K Spuds was a 2,800-acre potato farm just a few miles west of Pocatello. As I drove along the farm's perimeter, I could see a dark-red harvester churning up the ground, a side chute dropping potatoes into the back of an accompanying truck. I wondered why they still required migrant workers.

I finally came to the farm's entrance and pulled up to a metal building that was flanked by steel silos and three massive ridged steel hangars.

I parked the Chevy along the front of the building and got out. There was no one in sight, and I was starting to fear that Eddie wasn't there.

The office was about as austere as you'd expect from a potato farm. To one side of the room were two gray metal desks. There was a man sitting at one of them. He wore blue jeans and a green-and-red-plaid shirt with long sleeves and collar. His hair was snow white, though I guessed he was probably only in his early fifties. He looked up at me. "Can I help you?"

I walked to his desk. There was a copper-and-wood name plate on his desk: Dave.

"You're Dave."

"The same."

"My name is Charles. I'm looking for one of your migrant workers. His name is Eddie de la Cruz."

My request seemed to bother him. "Are you with ICE?"

Maybe it would have saved time if I'd just said "yes," but then he might have asked for my credentials.

"No. I'm a family friend."

"Just a moment." He typed something into his computer, then looked back at me. "We don't have a worker here by that name."

"You might not have record of him. He's undocumented."

I could see him tense at the word. "There are no undocumented workers here. The only migrant workers we employ are H-2A contract workers."

"That's not true," I said. "Because Eddie's not documented. And I know he's here."

The man just glared at me.

"Look, Dave. I'm not from Immigration. This is a personal matter. I just need to give Eddie an important message about his family, then I'll be gone."

"Why don't you just write something down, and if I happen to see someone by that name, I'll make sure he gets it."

"No," I said.

"Sorry, I can't help you." He turned away from me.

I looked at him for a moment, then said, "Okay." I lifted my phone and began searching the Internet. "There it is," I said softly. I started dialing a number.

"What are you doing?"

I stopped before dialing the last digit. "I'm calling the immigration office in Idaho Falls. If you can't help me, I'm sure they'll be happy to come check your employees."

"Your family *friend* will be deported."

"You just said my friend isn't here."

He just looked at me.

"I admit, this is new to me, but I'm guessing that these

immigration guys operate like most bureaucracies, and once they find a discrepancy, they start a full audit." I lifted the phone to my ear. "How much would something like that cost you?"

"Hang up," he said angrily. "Just hang up."

I put down my phone. "Yes?"

"They're out gleaning."

"Who?" I asked.

"The undocumented workers."

I nodded. "Where?"

"The far southwest pasture. There should be about twenty workers and a couple of white pickups."

"Thank you for your kind assistance," I said.

I drove the Malibu out over the freshly plowed field, which was kind of fun but would probably be frowned upon by the rental car company.

The pickup trucks were nearly half a mile from the office, surrounded by a few dozen migrant workers. I spotted Eddie about fifty yards out. He was wearing the same clothes he had on the last time I saw him, except they were dirtier, which I figured was a result of the potatoes. Like the rest of the workers he glanced up at me but continued working.

I parked my car about fifteen yards behind the first pickup, which was half-full of potatoes.

"Eddie!" I shouted.

Eddie looked up.

"Who are you?" the driver of the first truck asked.

"David sent me," I said. "I'm supposed to pick up Eddie."

Eddie took a few steps toward me. "Gringo?"

Ironically, he was the only one who had recognized me since I'd shaved.

I walked up to him and we embraced. "How are you, my friend?"

"You got my email," he said. "Have you come to work? This is much better work than the pigweed in Texas."

"No, I came to get you."

"Que?"

I opened the car's passenger door. "Come on, get in," I said. He just stood there looking at me. I gestured more firmly. "C'mon, Eddie. Get in. Now."

He walked over. I shut the door behind him, then climbed into the driver's seat. Eddie looked as confused as he was filthy. I spun the car around and headed back to the road.

"Where are we going, gringo? Where did you get a car?"

"You said you someday want to be with Felicia."

"I always want to be with Felicia."

"You're going to Miami to be with Felicia."

Eddie looked panicked. "No, no, no, gringo," he said. "It is not yet time for the orange harvest."

"I think you'll be okay."

We stopped in Pocatello to get a drink. I bought Eddie some *chicharróns* and a bottle of pineapple mango juice. As we drove from Pocatello I looked over at him. "Let me see your shirt," I said.

"My shirt?"

"Yes," I said. "The one you're wearing. Take it off."

Puzzled, he took off his shirt.

"Let me see it."

He handed it to me. I rolled down my window and threw it out.

"Gringo, my shirt."

"There's a T-shirt in the top of my bag," I said. "It doesn't have potatoes growing in it."

We spent the next hour discussing the new situation. It wasn't that he didn't understand what I was telling him, but that he didn't understand how it could be. Finally I said, "Do you know the word *rico*?"

"*Sí*," he said. "Rich."

"*Sí*. And I am *muy rico*."

Eddie shook his head. "Then why did you work in the fields?"

"I was pretending to be *pobre*."

"Why would you do that?"

"It was a joke," I said. "You know? *Broma*."

He shook his head. "I do not understand you, gringo."

"Don't worry about it," I said. "Do you have any identification?"

"Yes. I have this now." He pulled from his pocket a laminated identification card.

"That should do."

I called Amanda and had her arrange Eddie's flight to Miami and book two rooms at the Little America Hotel in downtown Salt Lake.

"Have you ever flown in an airplane before?"

He shook his head. "No, amigo."

I smiled. "Tomorrow's a whole new day for you."

Chapter Forty-Six

It's been more than a decade since I've seen my mother or father. I'm nervous to see both, but for very different reasons: him because of his failure; her because of mine.

CHARLES JAMES'S DIARY

We arrived back in Ogden around five. I parked the car in front of Michael's home, then said to Eddie, "We'll stay in Salt Lake City tonight. But I first need to stop and see my family."

"No worries, amigo. I am in no hurry."

Eddie walked with me to the front door, though I made him brush off his pants. I'm sure he was just glad that I didn't make him take them off.

"This is where I grew up," I said.

He looked around and nodded. "*Sí*. Very nice."

Everything's relative, I thought.

Before I could ring the doorbell, Mike opened the door.

"Welcome back."

"This is my friend Eddie."

"*Hola*, Eddie," Michael said. "*Que tal.*"

"Bastante bien. Y tu?"

"Come esta."

"You kept it up," I said. "Bravo."

"Wrong language," he said. "Come in, we're just about to make dinner."

Stacy walked out of the kitchen. "Hi, Charles." She looked at Eddie. "And you are?"

"This is my friend Eddie," I said.

"Welcome." She turned to Mike. "Should I throw in some more pasta?"

"We're having spaghetti," he said to me. "Join us."

"If it's not too much trouble," I said.

"It's spaghetti," Stacy said. "No trouble."

As we were finishing the meal, Mike asked, "So, big brother, what are your plans?"

"We're staying in Salt Lake tonight. Eddie has a morning flight to Miami."

"And you?"

"I'm headed back to Chicago."

"You're not going to see Mom and Dad?"

"I was thinking of seeing them on the way to Salt Lake."

"We'll go with you," Stacy said. "It's only twenty-five miles."

"All right," Mike said. "Let's go."

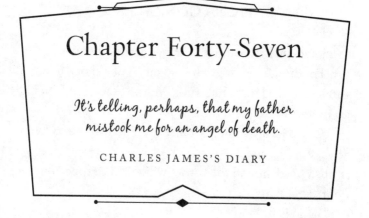

Chapter Forty-Seven

It's telling, perhaps, that my father mistook me for an angel of death.

CHARLES JAMES'S DIARY

The drive from Ogden to Bountiful was less than half an hour. The care facility my parents lived in looked new, with a stucco-and-vinyl-siding façade. It was nicely landscaped and built along a wide, flowing creek.

I invited Eddie to come in with us, but he insisted on staying in the car. I met Mike and Stacy in the care center's lobby.

"What floor are they on?" I asked.

"Two floors," Mike said. "Mom's in the assisted living, Dad's in the advanced care unit. We'll see Mom first."

We checked in at the front counter, then I followed Mike and Stacy to the elevator. We got out on the third floor and walked all the way down the hallway to the last door. It had a Plexiglas sign with my mother's name in it.

FIONA GONZALES

Someone had painted ladybugs around her name.

"I'm thinking it might be too much of a shock to her if you just walked in," Mike said. "Maybe Stacy and I should go in first and explain things."

"Good idea," I said. "I don't want to give her a heart attack."

I stepped around the corner while Mike rapped on the door.

"Who is it?"

"It's us, Mom. Stacy and Michael."

I could hear my mother fumble with the doorknob, then it finally opened. They all disappeared inside. I walked back out to the door. I had been standing there for maybe three minutes when I heard my mother scream, "Where?!"

The door flew open and my mother stood there looking at me in disbelief. Then she flung her arms around me. For the longest time she just said, "Thank you, Jesus. Thank you, Jesus. Thank you, Jesus."

We talked for nearly an hour. I could tell that Mike was getting tired, especially since he'd had so little sleep the night before. "It's getting late," he finally said.

"It's not late," my mother replied.

"Charles still hasn't seen Dad."

"Oh." My mother looked at me. "You need to see your father."

"It's pretty late," I said. "I could come back."

"No," she said. "You should see him tonight."

"I'll stay with Mom," Stacy said. "You boys go."

Mike and I took the elevator back down to the first floor. I followed Mike through some double doors, then down a tiled corridor. It was different from where my mother was staying. It felt more like a hospital than an apartment, which I supposed it was. Finally we stopped outside a door that was partially open.

"This is it," Mike said softly.

"You coming?" I asked.

He shook his head. "I think this is for you."

I pushed the door a little farther open and stepped inside. The room was small, with space enough for just one bed. The overhead lights were off and the room was lit only by a table lamp and the radiance of the room's monitors.

In the middle of it all was the shadowed figure of my father. *When did he get so small?* He was lying still, his eyes closed, his chest rising and falling, punctuated by an occasional squelch of oxygen from his tank. I noticed that his right hand was bandaged, and I could see where the stumps of his legs stopped short under the sheets. A catheter line ran out from his sheet to a plastic, urine-filled bag, and an oxygen tube ran up behind his head, where it split and circled his face. He was breathing heavily. Suddenly he cleared his throat and shuddered. I took another step closer.

"Is someone here?" his voice was hoarse and soft.

"It's me," I said.

He turned his head toward me. "Michael?"

I took a deep breath, then stepped closer. "No. It's Charles."

He was quiet a moment, then said, "Is it my time?"

It took me a moment to realize what he was thinking. "I'm not dead. There's been a mistake." I reached over and touched his arm. "I'm here."

I noticed something. A tear was snaking its way down his cheek. It was something I'd never seen before. "Why would you come to see me?"

I suppose it was a fair question. But I had a new answer. A real one. "I wanted to thank you."

He swallowed. "Why would you thank me?" He squinted, and now tears came from both eyes. "I was a bad father to you."

I couldn't believe what I was hearing. I just looked at him for a moment. For the first time in my life I felt no hatred for him. I felt only his pain.

"You had a hard life. But you made it possible for Mike and I to have a good one."

For a moment he was completely still, as if he'd fallen asleep. Suddenly he began to convulse slightly. At first I thought he was having a seizure or maybe even a heart attack. And then I realized that he was just crying.

Chapter Forty-Eight

For years I wondered what I would say if I ever saw my father again—never considering that words were not only insufficient, they were unnecessary.

CHARLES JAMES'S DIARY

I was with my father for nearly thirty minutes. We didn't talk. I just held his hand. Finally I leaned over and kissed him on the forehead. "Good-bye, Dad."

He clutched my hand, then let it go. I walked back out.

"How did it go?" Mike asked. He looked into my eyes, then said, "Like I said, he changed."

We walked back to my mother's room. I said good-bye to my mother, then walked out of the facility with Stacy and Mike.

"When are you coming back?" Mike asked.

"I don't know. I don't know what I'm going to do yet. You should come out to Chicago. I'll show you my town."

"I'd like that," Stacy said.

Mike and I hugged. "See you, brother," I said. "I'll call."

"I love you, man."

"I love you, too."

As I turned to go, Mike said, "It better not be another fifteen years."

I smiled. "It won't be fifteen days."

When I got back to my car Eddie was asleep. It was less than half an hour's drive to downtown Salt Lake City. Eddie woke before we reached the hotel. He sat up in his seat and looked around. "Where are we?"

"Salt Lake," I said.

"Bueno."

He followed me, wide-eyed, into the hotel's beautiful, spacious lobby. I checked us into our rooms, then I took him to his, which was just two doors down from mine. I had to show him how to use his magnetic key card.

He walked inside the room and then just stood there at the foot of his bed looking around. "This is where I sleep?"

"This is your room for tonight."

"This is like a king," he said.

"Enjoy," I said. I left him to his castle.

Chapter Forty-Nine

Fate has played its hand. A Joker went wild.

CHARLES JAMES'S DIARY

I knocked on Eddie's door the next morning at seven. He opened the door already dressed in the only clothes he had. He had probably slept in them.

"Let's get some breakfast," I said.

We ate downstairs in the hotel's buffet. Eddie wanted to take some of the food with him, which I stopped him from doing.

We still had ninety minutes, so I walked him over to City Creek Mall and bought him some new clothes and a bag to carry them in. I made him throw everything else he had away.

Then I took him to the airport, where I helped him get his boarding pass. On the way to security we stopped at an ATM and I took out five hundred dollars. I handed Eddie the money. "That's for expenses."

He looked stunned. I thought it was because I had just

given him so much money, but then he said, "The machine gives you money?"

I smiled. "Yes."

"You must show me how it works."

I walked him up to the security checkpoint. "I can't follow you past here," I said. "But you'll be fine. You're at gate C3; it's just straight ahead down that hall. Got it?"

He nodded.

"All right. Tell Felicia hi."

"Gringo."

"Yes?"

"You are the best man I know."

I just looked at him and said, "I'll see you in a few months. Now go."

I watched him walk through the checkpoint. He was like a child as the TSA officers told him what to do.

Once he was on the other side of the metal detector he turned back to me and waved. I waved in return. Then he turned and walked off toward the gate.

I was walking away from security when my phone rang.

"We have a problem," Amanda said.

Four words guaranteed to raise your blood pressure. "What is it?"

"Someone's filed a claim against your estate. They say they have a will."

"I didn't leave a will."

"He claims you wrote one. It has your signature and it's notarized."

"Who says that?"

"Glenn."

"Glenn Sperry?"

"Yes."

"If I wasn't so angry, I'd almost be impressed. I didn't think he had the ambition."

"Just greed," Amanda said.

"Did you call Doug?"

"Your lawyer? No."

"Why not?"

"Because he thinks you're dead."

"Then I'll call him," I said.

"Good luck," she said.

I hung up before realizing that I didn't know his number. I was about to call Amanda back when she texted the number to me.

I dialed the law firm. A mature female voice answered. "Good afternoon, Short Nelsen law offices." I always thought that they should change their firm's name, or at least invert the order of the partners' names. It sounded like the office for a vertically challenged attorney.

"Doug Short, please."

"May I tell him who's calling?"

"Tell him it's Charles James."

"Just a moment, Mr. James."

She put me on hold with a sprite minuet by Bach. A moment later she returned. "Mr. Short wants me to ask who this really is."

"I expected that. Ask him if he ever told his wife about New Orleans."

She put me on hold again. The minuet continued. A

moment later Doug's voice came on, cranky and gruff as usual. "What is this, extortion?"

"No, Dougy. I'm just getting your attention."

"Who is this?"

"It's me, Charles. I'm not dead."

"Is this a sick joke?"

"You sound like Amanda. The only sick joke I know is 'What do you call a hundred lawyers . . .'"

"A good start," he finished. "Prove you're Charles."

"Prove you're Doug," I said. "You don't recognize my voice?"

"You could be someone else."

"What do you want, DNA? We can call Amanda."

"She could be in on it."

"In on what?"

"What do you know about New Orleans?"

"You mean your discreet rendezvous that wasn't so discreet?"

"So James told someone."

"I never told anyone your secret, Dougy. Ask me something only I would know."

"What do I eat for breakfast?"

"Trick question. You don't eat breakfast; you have a 5-Hour Energy and then a steak with pommes frites at Bavette's for lunch."

He hesitated. "What's my dog's name?"

"Lady Dogiva."

He was quiet a moment, then said cautiously, "Charles?"

"In the flesh."

"What about the crash?"

"I checked in, but got off the flight before it took off."

"Why didn't you correct them?"

"I was trying to decide if I wanted to still be alive. Remember when I told you about that recurring dream I was having, the one where I was walking down a road. . . ."

". . . And fire was falling from the sky," he finished. "It really is you."

"I was having a spiritual crisis. When I realized that everyone thought I was dead, I decided to take some time off and figure things out."

"Amanda knows you're alive?"

"She's the only one who knows. Besides you and my family."

"This is so bizarre," he said. "I feel like I'm talking to a ghost."

"You are," I said. "So this is why I'm calling. Remember my salesman, Glenn Sperry?"

"No."

"Doesn't matter," I said. "He's a former employee who is now claiming that I left a will naming him as my sole beneficiary."

"How generous of you," Doug said. "Hold on, let me check the docket." I could hear him typing on his computer. After a few minutes he came back on. "Nothing in Cook County. Let me go deep on this. This the right number to call you back on?"

"You got it."

Twenty minutes later my phone rang. "Well, congratulations, Charles. You're officially dead."

"How did that happen?"

"A judge in DuPage County declared it. Your friend, Glenn Sperry, has filed a holographic will."

"What's a holographic will?"

"It's a handwritten will."

"Is that legal?"

"Legal is relative."

"Let me rephrase that. Could he win?"

"That depends on who's opposing it. And apparently it was notarized."

"So he found a high school buddy with a notary stamp. Isn't my son the legal heir?"

"Yes," he said. "Unless the will specifically disinherits him, which this apparently does."

"Scumbag," I said. "I'm surprised Monica hasn't filed for it."

"So far, this is the only challenge to your estate." He erupted in a fit of coughing, something he did frequently. When he returned he said, "Remember when Howard Hughes died, there was some weirdo who came forward claiming that he had once saved Hughes's life in the desert, so Hughes made him an heir to his fortune?"

"Dumar," I said. "Melvin Dumar."

"How did you know that?"

"I'm from Utah," I said. "They called it the Mormon Will."

"That was a holographic will."

"Like I asked before, could he win?"

"It's hard to prove, but you can't ignore it. And there's something a little dodgy about this. It's moving pretty quickly, and it looks like this Glenn dude is trying to fly under the radar. He might be getting some help. Why else would he file in DuPage?"

"I have no idea," I said.

"My guess is, he's friends with a judge somewhere who's on the take."

"Wait. We were having dinner once and Glenn told everyone that his sister-in-law's brother was a judge who got him out of speeding tickets."

"There you go," Doug said.

"What do we need to do?"

"First, I need to file a motion opposing probate. Of course, the easiest way to handle this is for you to just prove you're not dead."

"How do I do that?"

Doug laughed. "Remember that scene in the Monty Python *Holy Grail* movie? I'm not quite dead yet," he said in an English accent. He laughed. "You show up, my friend. You just show up."

"If I do, it's out. This will go public."

"That's the idea," Doug said. "It's that or lose it all. You and your son."

I breathed out heavily. "I guess it's time."

"I'll get started immediately. Where are you?"

"I'm in Salt Lake City."

"What are you doing there? Never mind. When will you be back in Chicago?"

"I'll fly out this afternoon."

Chapter Fifty

Word is out. Charles James lives.

CHARLES JAMES'S DIARY

I caught the first open flight from Salt Lake, landing in Chicago that evening around six. The last time I'd been in O'Hare the place was a morgue. Literally. Even more surreal: the gate where I disembarked was just one down from the gate Flight 227 had departed from. I walked past the gift shop where I had lost my bag. That same slow clerk was inside.

Amanda was waiting for me outside security. "How was the flight?"

"Better than my last Chicago flight."

"I should hope so. Did you check luggage?"

"One bag," I said.

We walked a ways down the terminal before Amanda said, "Well, the word is out."

"What word?"

"That Charles James lives."

I turned toward her. "Really?"

"There's already a media frenzy brewing. I'm getting flooded with interview requests."

"That fast."

"It just takes one match to start a forest fire."

"Who do you have?"

"In print, we've got interview requests from *USA Today*, the *Washington Post*, the *New York Times*, the *Wall Street Journal*, *Time* . . . all the players."

"What about TV?"

"*GMA*, *Today*, *CBS This Morning*. Pick a morning show; they all want you."

I turned back to the terminal. "I just want a nap."

We picked up my bag at the carousel, then got in to Amanda's car. I let her drive for a change. It was dark when she pulled into my driveway and shut off the engine. For a moment I just looked at my house.

Amanda glanced over at me. "How does it feel to be home?"

"Surreal."

I noticed one of the neighbors looking out their window. Amanda noticed, too. "Let's get you inside."

"You can go."

"I want to make sure everything's okay."

I retrieved my bag from the backseat, then walked up to the front door. I unlocked the door and walked inside. My burglar alarm started chirping. I just looked at it. I had forgotten my alarm code.

"Three-nine-eight-nine," Amanda said.

I punched in the number. "Thanks."

The room smelled stale, like old butter.

"Welcome home," Amanda said.

I set my bag down next to the stairway.

"I went grocery shopping yesterday so you'd have something to eat."

"Thank you."

I went to the sink and poured myself a glass of water, then sat up on the counter to drink it. Amanda just watched me. "This is hard for you, isn't it?"

"Being dead was less complicated."

For a moment we both just stood there. Then Amanda said, "Well, I'd better get on home. Tomorrow's going to be demanding. If you need anything, just call. We can talk about media in the morning."

"Good night," I said.

She was just opening the door. I said, "Amanda."

She turned back. "Yes?"

"Thank you for everything."

She smiled. "That's what I'm here for."

Chapter Fifty-One

The interview on GMA didn't go how I expected, which I should have expected, since I had no expectations. That doesn't make sense. We'll see how honesty plays out.

CHARLES JAMES'S DIARY

Amanda called early the next morning. "Are you ready?"

"I'm awake," I said. "Ready for what?"

"Your media."

"What am I looking at?"

"I've sent your schedule to your phone. Your first interview is with the *Washington Post* in twenty minutes. Then you're pretty much every thirty minutes until two fifteen, so you can dress and pack. I'll pick you up at two forty-five. Our flight's at five forty-five."

"Where are we going?"

"New York. You're on *Good Morning America* tomorrow at eight thirty."

I breathed out heavily. "There is no rest for the dead."

"That's the problem—you're not dead anymore. You've got fifteen minutes until your first interview. Go make yourself some toast. I got you some of that rye bread you like from Dinkel's."

"You're too good to me."

"I know. Now get going. You've got thirteen minutes. They'll be calling you on your cell."

The interviews went all day as planned. Amanda arrived early to help me pack. We flew out of O'Hare, landing in New York just a little after eight. We ate dinner at the Redeye Grill on Seventh Avenue. Amanda had to turn off her phone because it kept ringing. It seemed everyone wanted my story.

Amanda and I were in ABC's Times Square studio by six thirty the next morning, giving time for makeup. By seven forty-five we were sitting in the greenroom with politico Scott Rasmussen and one of the *Bachelorette* contestants waiting to go on.

"I did fourteen interviews yesterday," I said.

"Fifteen. You did one by text," Amanda said. "You're still getting calls. How many more interviews do you want?"

I looked at her. "None."

"None?"

"Stick a fork in me baby, I'm done."

She smiled. "I'll let them know. *GMA*'s not a bad way to go out."

A few minutes later a young intern wearing a blue ABC jacket walked into the room. "Mr. James?" she asked.

I raised my hand. "That's me."

"You're on next. Follow me, please."

"Good luck," Amanda said.

I followed the young woman down a narrow corridor to the studio. The *GMA* hostess was sitting on a couch talking to someone through her lapel mike. She looked over at me as I entered. "Good morning, Mr. James. Thanks for coming on the show."

"My pleasure," I said.

"Thirty seconds," the cameraman said.

"You've been making the rounds?" she asked.

"Pretty much."

"It's a big story," she said.

"Twenty seconds," a cameraman said.

The anchorwoman straightened her blouse and sat up, centering herself in her seat. "It's a really big story."

"Ten seconds. Nine, eight, seven, six . . ." The cameraman finished the countdown silently on his fingers. At zero he pointed at the anchor.

"Our next guest is the sole survivor of Chicago Flight 227, one of the most tragic aviation accidents in history. It was reported that two hundred twelve passengers and crew died on that flight. But just two days ago we learned that number was incorrect. There was one survivor: author and seminar host Mr. Charles James of Oak Park, Illinois.

"What makes Mr. James's story even more incredible

is that after he escaped death, he decided to go on a walk. Not just any walk: he walked the famous Route 66, nearly twenty-five hundred miles, from Chicago to Los Angeles." She turned back to me. "Charles, take us back to the afternoon of May third. What transpired that day to save your life?"

"I had just boarded the flight when I realized that I had left my laptop in one of the airport stores. I went out to retrieve it, and when I got back they had shut the Jetway door."

"Why didn't you tell someone that you had left the flight?"

"I tried. But it was one of those weather days at O'Hare when flights were running behind and the airline personnel were overwhelmed. Then, when I went to rebook my flight, my plane crashed and everything just shut down. So, after a while I just left the airport."

"Did you see any of the news coverage of the crash?"

"Of course. For days it's all there was."

"So you knew that you had been counted among the dead."

"Yes."

"Why didn't you come out publicly then?"

"A psychologist could probably answer that better than I could. Maybe it was survivor's guilt, but at the time I was going through a spiritual crisis. I took the experience as a sign to reexamine my life."

"By walking?"

"Yes. I've always believed that walking opens the mind to inspiration."

"Why Route 66?"

"I think it was symbolic. I started my career in Santa Monica, and it ended up in Chicago. Route 66 connects the two."

The woman's voice lowered. "Why do you think you lived when everyone else lost their lives?"

"I've wondered that every day since the crash. I don't know; maybe it's because only the good die young."

She chuckled.

"I didn't mean to sound flippant. There's nothing remotely amusing about any of this. But I'm pretty certain that everyone on that plane had more right to live than I did. Maybe it was simply grace that I was given time to wake up and do something positive with my life."

She seemed moved by my response. "You might say you've been given a second chance at life. If you could do one thing over, what would it be?"

I wasn't prepared for the question. Suddenly my eyes welled up. "I would have been the man my wife and son deserved."

"A beautiful answer. Thank you, Charles." She turned back toward the camera. "Back to you, Al."

"You did well," Amanda said as we walked out of the studio. "Maybe the best interview you've ever done on national TV."

"I had nothing to sell," I said. I turned to her. "I just want to go home."

We landed at O'Hare a little after 5:00 p.m. Amanda had left her car at the airport, but she was as exhausted as I was, so I called an Uber and sent her home. "Take the day off," I said. "I don't want to hear from you until Thursday."

"Promise," she said. She kissed me on the cheek. "Good job today."

When I reached home I went straight to bed. I felt like the past had finally caught up to me. I slept for eighteen hours, waking around one the next afternoon. I didn't even turn my phone on.

Honestly, I wasn't sure what to do with myself. Finally I put on my shorts and went out walking. I planned to walk a few miles but ended up walking eight, all the way to the Garfield Park Conservatory and back.

I then read for a few hours, made myself some spaghetti with mizithra cheese for dinner, and went back to bed.

I woke the next day at noon. I turned on my phone. Amanda had called three times.

My phone rang just twenty minutes after I turned it on.

"Did you sleep?" Amanda asked.

"Yeah. Almost eighteen hours Tuesday night. Twelve last night."

"It's finally caught up to you."

"So what's going on in the world?"

"Doug called yesterday afternoon. He said that in light of all the media, the judge in DuPage canceled your death certificate. He said the claim has been redacted and the concerned parties are running like cockroaches in sunlight."

"That's good news. Anything else?"

"Yes. He asked if you wanted to step on the cockroaches."

I grinned. "No. But I will be paying Glenn a visit."

"Lucky him."

Just then my doorbell rang. "Someone's here."

"You better get that," she said, sounding uncharacteristically eager. "You can call me later."

"All right. I'll call you back." She hung up first, which was also unusual. *What was that about?* I thought.

I pulled on my sweats and a Chicago Bulls tank top and walked downstairs. *Probably a water-purifier salesman*, I thought. I opened the door. Monica was standing on my front porch.

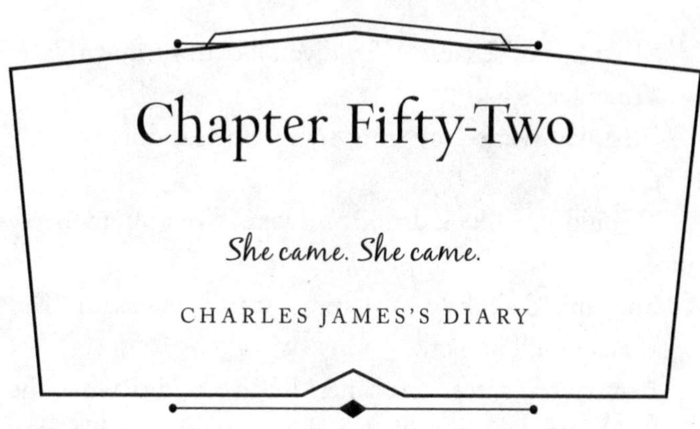

Chapter Fifty-Two

She came. She came.

CHARLES JAMES'S DIARY

I must have stared at her for at least a minute. She looked older, of course, but even more beautiful than I remembered. She still looked like the woman I had once fallen in love with.

After a moment she said, "Hi."

"Hi," I returned.

She waited another moment, then said, "May I come in?"

"Sorry. Of course," I said, stepping back.

She stepped inside. I shut the door behind her.

"How did you find me?" I asked.

"Amanda."

That explained Amanda's behavior.

Monica glanced around the room. "You have a beautiful home."

"It's too big for just me."

"It's nice."

"Thank you," I said. "Would you like to sit down?"

"Yes, please."

I led her over to my front room. She sat down on my sofa.

"Would you like a drink?" I asked. "I've got cranberry juice."

She smiled slightly. "You remembered," she said. "But no, thank you. I'm okay."

I sat down across from her. I had no idea what she wanted. During my walk I had spent uncountable moments fantasizing about how surprising my appearance on her doorstep would be, only to have it the other way around.

"How are you?" she asked.

"I'm alive. At least that's what the media's saying. 'Course, you never know, with all the fake news these days." She didn't smile. "But I guess you knew that."

"I saw you on TV Tuesday. You were on one of the morning shows."

"There's been a lot of interest in my story."

Monica went quiet. She looked vulnerable.

"How have you been?" I asked.

She shrugged. "Gabriel's good. He's doing amazing in school. He's smart like his dad."

I grinned. "That's a low bar."

She just looked at me. "You've changed."

I didn't know how to respond to that. She leaned forward. "Amanda told me about all you've been doing. The shelter in Albuquerque, the waitress, the farmworker . . ."

She was quiet for a moment, then said, "You came by the house. Didn't you?"

I nodded slowly. "How did you know?"

"Gabriel said a nice man came by. When I saw you on TV I knew it was you." She breathed out. "Or maybe I just hoped."

"You hoped it was me?"

She looked even more vulnerable. She took a deep breath. "What you said on TV. About second chances. Did you mean that?"

"I'm sorry, I didn't mean to embarrass you. I know you're getting married . . ."

For a moment she looked down as if gathering her thoughts. Then she looked back up. "The thing is . . ." She sighed heavily. "When I heard you died, I thought it would be best for Gabriel to have a man around. You know, like a father."

"Brilliant," I said, nodding slowly. "That's smart. That's good for him." I looked down for a moment as a wave of pain spread over me. Then I slowly looked up at her. "And you?"

For a moment she didn't move. Then she exhaled slowly. "I guess I was hoping for something else."

I didn't understand. "Something?"

"Someone." She looked up. "Did you really just walk two thousand miles?"

"More than that, actually."

"That's a long way to walk."

"Very."

She looked deeper into my eyes and asked softly, "Why?"

I just looked into her eyes, and for a moment the miles and years and heartache vanished. There was only her and me and something we both wanted.

"I guess when you're looking for the right pearl, you don't care how far you have to go."

Her eyes filled with tears, then suddenly her mouth rose in a sweet, simple smile. "I think you just found her."

Chapter Fifty-Three

Don't give up. Everyone who got to where they are had to start from where they were.

CHARLES JAMES'S DIARY

Mount Elbert, Colorado. 14,400 feet above sea level.

It took me a little less than two hours to reach the top of Mount Elbert. I'm told that's not bad, especially for a rookie climber, but I did just walk two thousand miles.

The hike up was steep and rocky and the summit was mostly barren, just hard dirt with shale-like stones gathered in sharp, craggy piles. But when I looked around me, there was the most beautiful view. The experience reminded me of my life.

As I climbed the mountain, I had passed at least a dozen people coming down, and I was glad to find myself alone at the summit. I wanted the time by myself with McKay.

I found the brass survey marker that had been embedded in stone by the US Coast and Geodetic Survey, marking the high point of Colorado. Rocky mountain high. Reminded me of that John Denver song.

I took the stainless-steel cremation canister out of my backpack and set it on the brass marker. Metal on metal.

"Well, old man, I hope you appreciate this; you're back on top again." I grinned. "You're kind of a captive audience right now, so before I let you go, I have a few things I need to get off my chest. First, I want to thank you for your advice and let you know that I did what you said. I did my heart song. Just like those aboriginals you were talking about. It took a plane crash to get me there, but I did it.

"But you already know that, don't you? Maybe you even walked a few of those miles with me. I wouldn't be surprised. You paved the way for me my whole life."

A light breeze passed. I closed my eyes and listened to it as it whistled by. I took another deep breath. "You were right. You told me to '*Ditch the past and be someone else.*' That's what you said. What you never told me was that if I ditched my past, something better would find me. The past I hoped for. It all came back. I even got a second chance. Maybe you had something to do with that, too."

I looked down at the canister. "You know, you weighed more than I thought you would. Almost six pounds. The guy at the crematorium said it's not the weight but the height that makes the difference. I guess fat just evaporates. If only we could have sold that from the stage, right?

"I hope you don't mind, but I had this made out of you." From beneath my shirt I lifted the gold rope that had once held Monica's ring. Now it held a single diamond in a gold setting. "When we first met, you called me a diamond in the rough. So I had you made into one. They can do that now. They've got a machine that turns your ashes into a diamond. They call them cremation diamonds. People will do anything for a buck, right? But I thought it was kind of cool. The guy there said to make them they need to create almost a million pounds of pressure per square inch.

"In one of your presentations, you used to talk about how diamonds were made from pressure, heat, and time. You said that's how winners are made, too, right? You were right about that."

I put the gem back under my shirt. "I had Marissa's permission to make it, of course. Actually, I had one made for her, too. She told me that she was going to have a ring made from it so she could keep you close. I told her you'd rather be a necklace than a ring. Better view. She laughed at that."

I took a thin towel out of my backpack and laid it out flat, then screwed the lid off the canister.

"I know it's not you in there. A bunch of ashes. You were more than carbon. You were energy. And energy can't be destroyed. So you're somewhere. That gives me hope." I poured the ashes into the center of the towel. "One more thing. You said at my funeral that you wished your sons had known me. They will. I'll look over them. I promise. Don't worry, if they ever need anything, I'll be there. For Marissa, too. Most of all, I'll let your boys know what a great man you were."

I breathed out slowly. "Oh, one more thing. If you're

doing your thing up there, keep the audience warm. When I get there, I might have something to say."

I closed my eyes and listened until there was another strong breeze. Then I grabbed the towel by its four ends and threw it high in the air. The towel opened in the wind, the ashes spreading out in the air like a soft cloud until they were gone. "See you later, pal."

I sat for just a minute more, then returned the canister to my backpack and headed back down the mountain to my wife and son.

Epilogue

A FINAL NOTE FROM RICHARD

I've always hated it when a speaker shares a beautifully inspired message, only to be followed by some well-meaning but clumsy "post speaker" who tries to synthesize the message with his own, less enlightened take. I say let it stand.

So be it. I have little more to add to Charles's story than an epilogue of the events that followed.

Charles and Monica were remarried on October 11 of that year in Ogden, Utah. Gabriel, Mike and Stacy, Monica's father, and Charles's mother were there. Charles's father wasn't. He passed away just nine days after Charles visited him in the care center.

Amanda was there, of course, running the show, along with her new best friend, Marissa, and her two sons.

I was there, too—not to take notes but to celebrate their miracle. I don't think I've ever seen a happier couple. Monica tells me that the first thing Charles says to her each morning is "How can I make your day better?"

Marissa told us that Eddie and Felicia are doing well and that Felicia is expecting a girl next March. Eddie is in the process of applying for US citizenship. I've talked to him. He remains grateful for all Charles has done for him.

For the sake of transparency, I confess that I've had trouble verifying some aspects of Charles's story, for two reasons: First, because many parts of his accounting, obviously, are unverifiable. He, like the rest of us, took his journey alone. I couldn't have been there in his hotel room any more than I could be in his mind.

The second reason is that I've had trouble holding Charles down long enough to fact-check. Charles is jealous with his family time, and the James family has been traveling a lot, making up for lost years. But from what I've seen, Charles has been impeccable with his word. Gabriel is friends with McKay's two sons, but more than that, every time I've seen him, he's been with his father. The last time I saw him he was following his father around the house, shouting into a plastic microphone. I wouldn't be surprised to see the gift pass on.

In the time I've shared with him, I've pressed Charles in a dozen different ways to tell me what it is that he learned from his journey. He has cleverly resisted. It took me a while to understand why—his discovery belongs to him. I think he wanted those who read his story to discover for themselves what it is that they learned.

So this is what I've taken from his walk, summed up in a simple yet ironic statement: to lose your life is to find it. That's it. The greatest self-interest is, simply, an interest in others.

Charles's story is one of redemption—my favorite kind of story. I think it's most people's favorite kind of story, too. Perhaps because in the telling we have hope that maybe we, too, can be redeemed.

In my decades of writing I've found that the best stories come full circle. Charles James's story did just that. More important, so did his life. The last I heard, he had moved back from Chicago to California. I don't think he walked.

Acknowledgments

I am grateful for my ever-wonderful agent, Laurie Liss, and the Simon & Schuster team that has walked with me for all these years: Jonathan Karp, Carolyn Reidy, and Richard Rhorer.

I'm grateful for my new team at Gallery: Jennifer Bergstrom, my new editor Lauren McKenna (don't say I didn't warn you), Maggie Loughran, Abby Zidle, Jean Anne Rose, Jennifer Long, and Caitlyn Reuss.

My staff; my talented daughter, bestselling author Jenna Evans Welch (thank you for stepping in even when your own books needed you); Barry Evans; and Heather McVey. Thank you, Diane Glad, for traveling Route 66 with me.

Also, thank you to Don Nicholson from the Salt Lake Rescue Mission, for your research assistance and all the good you do; Eric "Cowboy" Burson, for research under the viaduct and for feeding the homeless; and Kelly Glad, for your technical help and your Spanish translations (I look forward to reading your book one day). A big thank-you to Julie Shigekuni, for dinner, hospitality, and a very funny story in Albuquerque, and to Pastor Paul Robie, for your beautiful insight.

And always, Keri. I couldn't live without you, my love.

About the Author

RICHARD PAUL EVANS is the #1 bestselling author of *The Christmas Box* and the Michael Vey series. Each of his more than thirty-five novels has been a *New York Times* bestseller. There are more than thirty-five million copies of his books in print worldwide, translated into more than twenty-four languages. Seven of his novels have been turned into television movies. He is the recipient of numerous awards, including the American Mothers Book Award, the Romantic Times Best Women's Novel of the Year Award, the German Audience Gold Award for Romance, five Religion Communicators Council Wilbur Awards, the Washington Times Humanitarian of the Century Award, and the Volunteers of America National Empathy Award. He lives in Salt Lake City, Utah, with his wife, Keri, not far from their five children and two grandchildren.